LIFEMOBILE

LIFEMOBILE

by

JONATHAN RINTELS

PROSPECTA PRESS

FSC
www.fsc.org

MIX
Paper from
responsible sources
FSC® C004071

ANCIENT FOREST™
FRIENDLY

For J.B. and Ciaccia,
my two Lifemobiles

LIFEMOBILE

CHAPTER 1

Four decades after I thought I had buried it, the hated, humiliating word had thrust up from my brain's subconscious like Carrie's hand from the grave. It spun around and rolled over, crashing against the walls of my skull, out of control, just like the unsafe car it described. It was that word my wise-guy buddies gleefully taunted whenever their vigilant ears detected the ringing pistons straining within the air-cooled aluminum engine in my father's 1965 Chevrolet Corvair. Hiding in the bushes, my friends would lie in wait, giggling, until our sky-blue four-door huffed and puffed around the corner, its 110 rear-mounted horses struggling to push Dad and the other three middle management men in his carpool up the steep hill to our house. Suddenly, at the point of maximum breakaway danger, as the Corvair's heavy tail swung around the bend and its whining engine reached full thrust, just when its tires would surely and catastrophically lose grip with the road, the guys leaped out from behind the shrubbery, shrieking in terror that word, that awful mocking jeer: "DEATHMOBILE!"

Because you just never knew when a Corvair might suddenly spin, or roll, or veer out of control and chase you down the sidewalk, murder on its mind. "RUN FOR YOUR LIVES!" the guys hollered in mock panic, diving behind brick walls or climbing up oak trees, anything to escape my father's cherished example of America's Killer Car.

The Corvair was General Motors' infamous compact car built from 1960 to 1969—all 10 years of America's counter-cultural Sixties—and it ran counter to almost everything that had preceded it in America's car culture. Many remember it as the car that had the trunk in the front, the air-cooled aluminum engine in the rear, the oil on the ground, the roof on the road, and the wheels in the air after rolling over like a puppy wanting its belly scratched. Famously dubbed "unsafe at any speed" by then-unknown Ralph Nader in his 1965 best-seller, the Corvair had a homicidal reputation on the highway that remains unrivaled among American automobiles, with the possible exception of Stephen King's *Christine*.

Of course, my father wasn't the only fan of the Corvair. Elvis Presley bought one for his new wife, Priscilla. Before he became Muhammad Ali, Cassius Clay owned a Corvair. How completely cool was my dad driving me around in the same car owned by Elvis and Cassius Clay? Very Cool—until Corvairs became known as Deathmobiles. Then it became Absolute Zero Cool.

For over a week now, the peaceful sheep I tried to conjure in my mind to help me fall asleep kept morphing into Corvairs in a slow-motion ballet, pirouetting around the corner of my old street, then rolling over, bursting into flame, and detonating in elegant mushroom clouds. For four decades, I had barely given a thought to our Corvair, and now I could think of nothing else. As the dawn's early light filtered through the window blinds, I saw in my mind my buddies run from our blazing Deathmobile. Then came a secondary explosion. Followed by a third. Wait—I was wide awake. These explosions were real.

I reached the TV room downstairs just as the booming explosions ended and heard my son's flat and booming voice:

Stalking Denny Hamlin down the back straightaway at Talladega, Benjy Bennett, the talented rookie who had taken NASCAR by storm this season, knew he had a lot of car under him. But he didn't care to share that information with the rest of the race world. Hamlin's car looked tight, as if it wanted to kiss the wall at nearly 200 miles per hour. Bennett set him up for the pass out of Turn Four. As Hamlin's Toyota punched a hole in the air ahead of him, Bennett latched onto the pull of the draft that the absence of air resistance had suddenly created. As if fired from a cannon, Bennett's car exploded forward. An almost imperceptible turn of the wheel dropped him down low so that he didn't smash Hamlin's tail. In a blink, Bennett had the nose of his car underneath Hamlin's.

I entered the TV room. Benjy was rocking in his video game chair with the boom box speakers by his ears, staring intently at the video-game racing drama unfolding on the television screen. His long legs and size 13 feet pushed back and forth off the floor like the pistons of a NASCAR engine. His brown Beatles haircut and high school senior's wispy peach fuzz made him resemble a young George Harrison; he loved to listen to my old Beatles vinyls and soak up every photo and word on the worn album covers, so this was perhaps not a coincidence. Focusing so intently on the video game that he might melt the screen, repeating a story he authored about racing Denny Hamlin at Talladega, he still hadn't acknowledged me. For three years, he had played this same game at the same time each morning, repeating the same story almost word for word. I knew it by heart.

NASCAR drivers face hundreds of instantaneous life-or-death decisions in every race. Making those decisions correctly is what separates the NASCAR champs from the also-rans, and the dead. Benjy Bennett faced one of those decisions right now, and he and Hamlin both knew it. He refused to back off. Instead, he pressed the accelerator, demanding every ounce of power his 358 cubic inch, 810 horsepower V-8 engine could deliver. He held his line around the turn, leaving Hamlin outside him, and took the lead. But instead of falling in quietly behind the upstart rookie, Hamlin tapped his right rear fender. For every rookie driver, there's a first time for everything, and this was Benjy Bennett's first time to try and keep from dying at Talladega.

I had no idea where Benjy came up with this stuff. We had never been to a NASCAR race. We rarely watched racing on TV. Yet Benjy had created this nail-biting drama years earlier when he first became fascinated and possessed by this video game. Now came my favorite part, where his prose got positively purple:

Suddenly, Bennett had lost the down force caused during high-speed racing when superfast air pressed down against the car's front and rear wings. Without that precious down force, the car was light on its tires, and without tires firmly on the pavement, the cocky kid was not driving a car but piloting an out-of-control missile. Bennett had never flown a missile before, but that didn't stop him. He coolly held on to bring it in for a safe landing on the Talladega asphalt, somehow still facing forward down the back straightaway.

Benjy thought he knew the difference between luck and skill, and he knew that saving his car and his life had been pure, unadulterated luck. Now, his skill kicked in. He punched the accelerator. Suddenly, he was in first place, and he wasn't about to give it back.

"Morning," I greeted my son as the story wrapped. "Sleep okay?"

"Fine," Benjy replied. "Dad, do you think we will ever end poverty in America?" As he awaited my answer, he climbed out of his rocker and shut off the game. Suddenly, he was half a foot taller than me and staring down, deep into my foggy eyes.

"Uhhhhh," I stalled, trying to wake my brain cells from their torpor. "Sorry, but I haven't had coffee yet. What was the question again?"

Benjy then repeated the question, word for insistent word, while purposefully pacing, his long strides taking him back and forth across the room like a caged cougar. Sure, it was early, but I should have been prepared. For the past decade, my son had started almost every day not with a "Good Morning," but with a Big Picture 10,000-word essay question. Usually, he answered it himself, before I had a chance, and today was no exception. "I think technology will help end poverty in America," Benjy declared. "Technology will help deliver more food and stuff people need at lower cost. And education will provide more opportunity. More people will be able to go to college." He paused briefly, then asked, "Dad?"

I braced myself for another Big Question.

Benjy stopped pacing and turned to face me. "Do you remember Riley?"

Riley? I'd heard the name, but drew a blank. Someone involved in ending poverty?

"In *National Treasure*. Remember?"

Oh, now I got it. We'd changed the subject and I'd missed it. "Okay, I remember. Riley was..." But then I didn't remember. "Benjy, I'd like to make some coffee," I finally pleaded.

"Riley is Ben Gates's best friend and assistant, Dad!" Benjy said, frustrated by my obliviousness. *National Treasure* and its sequel were two of Benjy's favorite movies—he loved the combination of history, fantasy, and whodunit. I'd seen them with him so often that I knew them almost as well as he did. My failure to identify Riley was an unforgivable lapse.

As Benjy paced, his right hand flapped compulsively as if he were dribbling an imaginary basketball. "They say in the movie that he's Irish. Do you think he's Irish?" His hand beat down on each syllable.

Now I was on firmer footing. Even without the benefit of coffee, I recalled our endless viewings of the two *National Treasure* films. "He has Irish ancestors, I think. It's common for people to be identified by their heritage, even though I'm sure he is an American."

"But they say he's Irish. How can they say he's Irish if he's American? They're not telling the truth."

"It's not that they're lying, Benjy. It's just a way some Americans identify themselves—by where their family is originally from. Almost all Americans' ancestors came here from another country. Right?"

"But they say he's Irish!" Benjy insisted. "And you're saying he's American!"

"Benjy, I think I answered your question. It's just a way people talk about their heritage. I have German heritage, your mother had Scottish. So you're half German, half Scottish."

"No, you're confused, Dad. I'm American because I was born here. And Riley was born in America, so he's American. I think they should correct that. People could get confused."

"I'm going to the kitchen and getting coffee," I declared. A child like Benjy with Asperger's Syndrome, sometimes referred to as "high-functioning autism," often fixates and perseverates. Sometimes "Aspies" obsess about superheroes, or trains, or video games, but it can be anything. One of Benjy's many obsessions was "truth-telling." If someone called Riley "Irish," then Riley darn well better have an Irish passport or Benjy locked onto the divergence from the truth like a shark on wounded prey, shaking and thrashing the inconsistency until either he lost interest or the prey died.

Half an hour later, Benjy and I waited at the end of the driveway for the school bus. He paced back and forth across the asphalt, speaking to himself and flapping his hand, while I read the newspaper. For years,

I had criticized his pacing and hand-flapping and self-talking, and demanded that he stop. He never did. He said he couldn't. "Even if it looks odd, if he doesn't do that stuff, he might explode," his mother, Annie, would tell me, trying to ease my anger and frustration. "You can't change him," she'd say again and again. "He'll change you."

But Annie had died two years earlier, after a seemingly routine case of the flu turned into a whole-body sepsis infection. Somehow, when I lost her, I also lost the will to battle Benjy constantly over his quirky behavior. I didn't want our constant battling to drive him away—or drive us both crazy—so I tried to keep quiet. But just as I hadn't changed him, he hadn't changed me either. I was still angry and frustrated. I still worried what the future would hold for him if he couldn't change.

"You checked everything off your Before School list. Right?" I prodded. It was a question that almost always made him stop pacing to answer.

He stopped pacing. "Yes."

"And the Homework Assignment List?" The lists were one of Annie's wonderful strategies to keep Benjy on task and organized.

"Yes, Dad," he said, annoyed, then changed the subject to another of his favorite topics. "Dad, I don't want to ride the short bus anymore."

"Then I'll have to drive you to school," I said, as I said most days.

"No. I want to ride the long bus," he insisted. "The so-called 'normal' bus."

"We tried that, as you will recall," I said, as I said most days.

"They bullied me because I'm different," he vented. "It's the bullies who have a disability, not me. I should not be penalized and stigmatized for their bad behavior. They should ride the short bus, not me. They should call it the Bully Bus."

"Benjy, the short bus does not stigmatize you. It is…"

"Yes, it does," he interrupted. "It's for people with disabilities. I don't like that label. I'm just different. All the kids on my bus are just different. We can do anything, we just do it differently. Why do we have to be labeled as disabled?"

"I agree, you can do anything you set your mind to," I continued, as I continued most days. "But some of the kids need specially trained personnel and equipment. And look at the bright side. You get door-to-door service and it gets you to school in half the time."

"I can't wait to get to Wheeler," Benjy said. "They don't have short buses or bullies."

Lots of high school graduates with Asperger's successfully attend traditional colleges, most of which have offices and support services for students with disabilities. But for Benjy, who could pace and recite for hours if no one intervened, and who had significant challenges organizing himself, Wheeler College in North Carolina was a perfect fit. In fact, it was the only fit. Wheeler was the only college program specifically designed for students with severe Asperger's that taught independent living skills as well as academics, and was within driving distance of our home—something Annie and I had both insisted on in case Benjy suddenly needed a parent to support him.

Benjy opened the mailbox and peered inside. "The post office didn't deliver the envelope yet."

I checked my watch. "Benjy, the post office isn't even open yet, and we picked up yesterday's mail when you got home from school. So the envelope from Wheeler couldn't possibly be here."

"If the post office delivered the envelope to the wrong house, and the person at the wrong house then put it in our box, it could be here."

"You got me," I conceded, as I always did at this point in our daily discussion. "But Wheeler told us they wouldn't send out their acceptance letters for almost another month."

"They could send them earlier," he said.

The short bus turned the corner and stopped at our driveway, and its door opened wide. "I don't need help," Benjy barked at Mavis, the specially trained assistant, as he did every day when she got off the bus to assist him. "I'm just different."

Fortunately, Mavis had Annie's patience—it was part of her training—and she genially accepted Benjy's flouting of the social niceties. "It's just the procedure we follow, Benjy, you know that," she said, as she said almost every day. "Did you give those NASCAR drivers another racing lesson they'll never forget?"

"That's just a game," Benjy complained, as he did every day. "I have to play a game about driving because I'm not allowed to drive for real. The DMV discriminates against people who are different."

"See ya this afternoon, dude," I told Benjy, waving. "Learn lots and lots, okay?"

Without answering, Benjy sat on the opposite side of the bus and gazed out the far window. Prompted by Mavis, he turned to me, enthusiastically waved back, then turned away to gaze again out the window.

CHAPTER 2

A ha! Now I understood why memories of the Deathmobile were careening all over my brain. It was because suddenly the Corvair was all over the news. Toyota Camrys with stuck accelerators were running out of control, causing accidents and even fatalities. Respected auto industry analysts asked whether the Camry was to Toyota what the dangerous Corvair had been to General Motors—a deadly disaster that could so devastate Toyota that it might ultimately go bankrupt, just as General Motors had recently—and humiliatingly—been bankrupted.

Wow. Fifty years after its introduction and 40 years after its demise, the Corvair was being blamed for slaying the mighty multinational corporation that had spawned it. It was still the Killer Car! No wonder I hadn't seen a Corvair in years. GM and the government couldn't possibly allow what Nader called the "one-car accident" to continue to endanger the public; they must have banned the car from the public highways and crushed every one they could find. I wondered if that had happened when Dad was alive. I wondered if he'd heard. He'd driven me in his Deathmobile to all those Little League practices and games, and the Civil War battlegrounds he loved to tour. Did he know he had put our family in mortal danger?

I put aside the software manual I was writing for a longtime client. Ordinarily, I had a strict rule against surfing the net during work time, but now I typed in "Corvair." Google took .58 seconds to retrieve "about 9,460,000 search results" on the Internet. The top-ranked links included the Corvair Society of America ("CORSA, 4,800 members and 125 local chapters worldwide"); Clark's Corvair Parts ("world's largest Corvair parts supplier, over 15,000 Corvair parts in stock!"); a Wikipedia entry (14 chapters!); several forums and sites dedicated to buying, selling, maintaining, celebrating, defending, lambasting, and lampooning Corvairs; a site describing the use of Corvair engines to power airplanes (huh? I had always thought Corvair engines leaked oil and were unreliable); a "Sexy '65 Corvair TV Commercial" (as hot Swedish blonde runs toward camera, a gravel-voiced announcer intones, "You are about to meet a true international beauty, with a shape that blends elegance with excitement. Corvair for 1965!" Camera leaves hot Swedish blonde and pans to the Corvair); and a *Time* magazine article, "The 50 Worst Cars of All Time" (after recapping Nader's charges, the author concluded, "Even so, my family had a Corvair, white with red interior, and we loved it.").

Across the Internet, I watched Corvairs ford rushing rivers; slog through jungle mud; churn through waist-deep snow; and sway confidently through the cones of an auto slalom. I listened to a song by a band named Microbunny called "Evergrowing Rust on a 1967 Corvair." I watched a video of *Tonight Show* host Jay Leno, one of America's foremost Car Guys, merrily cruising down the Pacific Coast Highway in his meticulously restored '66 Corvair turbo as he extolled the rear-engine, air-cooled "American Porsche." It turned out he owned a bunch of Corvairs. In another *Tonight Show* video, as Leno touted the car to Sylvester Stallone, the bewildered star of *Rocky* stared at him wide-eyed, not knowing whether to laugh or call a doctor.

So which was the Corvair? A Deathmobile? An American Porsche? Both? Neither? How could one car still stir up such conflicting passions decades after it disappeared from the highways?

But, in fact, it turned out that lots of Corvairs were still on America's highways. With price tags ranging from a high of tens of thousands of dollars to a low of "free to the first person who gets this [expletive deleted] thing out of my sight," anybody could buy a Corvair. So if these cars were so widely available, and so frequently driven, how could they be so unsafe? Were these Corvair owners outlaws? Suicidal? It didn't make sense.

"Hi, Dad." In all the hours that Benjy had been at school, I'd been so fixated on Corvairs that I hadn't once left the computer, not even to answer the Call of Nature.

"Hey, dude, how was it?" I answered wearily, blinking my strained eyes.

"Good," he replied, scrutinizing me closely.

"What's wrong?" I asked.

"Your eyes are red," Benjy informed me. "Mom said I have to take a break from the computer every twenty minutes. You should set a timer like I do."

"You're right. I got mesmerized by something."

"You should take breaks. You tell me not to get mesmerized."

"I know. I should take my own advice."

"You forgot to bring the mail in." He handed it to me. "The letter from Wheeler didn't come."

"Not for several more weeks, they said. They've got several finalists to interview."

"Okay."

Benjy and I had first toured Wheeler's classic ivy-covered brick campus back in the fall as the leaves were changing. The school boasted excellent communications programs that attracted Benjy; after he graduated, he wanted to advocate for people with "differences," as he called them. The tightly clustered campus in a small town would help him avoid getting lost. He could have his own dorm room, which meant his hand-flapping, pacing, and reciting would not bother a roommate. There were counselors trained to help students like him with meals, laundry, medications, and social activities. It all seemed perfect for him. In the months that followed our visit, he interviewed repeatedly with the Asperger's program staff. Meeting so many people who actually "got" Benjy, with all his gifts and quirks and challenges, and who would dedicate themselves to helping him succeed—it's no wonder we'd both fallen in love with the place.

"You're a great candidate, but anything can happen, so don't get your hopes up too high. Community college is also a great option, and you can live at home." With his grades and credentials, I thought he was a lock to get in to Wheeler. He had already been told he was a finalist. Still, don't count your chickens...

"You're repeating yourself, Dad," he said, annoyed. "You always tell me not to repeat myself, but you're repeating yourself. You say that every time we talk about Wheeler. I want to go there. I'm nineteen years old. I don't want to live with you the rest of my life."

He marched upstairs to his room to do his homework.

Asperger's Syndrome, according to most experts, is transmitted through the genes, usually down the male line. This hypothesis rang painfully true to me; all I had to do was look in the mirror. Neither Annie nor I had heard of Asperger's before Benjy was diagnosed with it. Yet even before we learned about it, whenever I might criticize Benjy's obsessions and lack of social niceties, Annie would murmur to me, "You're not exactly Honor Roll at Charm School yourself, you know." She was right; I took a back seat to no one, not even Benjy, on lack of social graces. And my Corvair compulsion left no doubt where Benjy's obsessive behavior originated. After fetching a cup of coffee and a plain donut, I returned to my computer. Google claimed there were still over nine million Corvair search results I hadn't yet investigated. I was just getting started.

"Did the letter from Wheeler come today?" Benjy asked at the very same time the next day. He was standing in my office door, just home from school. I hadn't heard him come in.

"Benjy, when it comes, you'll be the first to know."

"Okay." He looked me over carefully.

"Are my eyes red again?" I asked. He nodded. I'd blown another whole day staring at the computer monitor in my deep dive into the mysteries of the Corvair. "Pull up a chair," I invited. "I've been research-ing Grandpa's old car. Did he ever talk to you about his Corvair?"

"He mostly talked about Dartmouth College," Benjy said, stretch-ing out his long legs as he slouched in the chair. "He wanted me to go there, but I'm not. Even though I told him I would. I didn't know I had Asperger's then."

"Benjy, if Grandpa were here, he'd be incredibly proud of everything you've accomplished, okay? Dartmouth was his college, he really loved it, and he wanted me to go there, too. But I didn't; I chose the school that was best for me, and so will you. Really, don't worry about that Dartmouth stuff. He was very old when he told you that and not thinking clearly. And he didn't know you had Asperger's either."

Benjy shrugged. I couldn't tell whether I'd persuaded him. "He was a good reciter," Benjy, who was such a World Class Reciter, recalled. "He knew lots of good books and poems." When Benjy was three years old, he recited from memory to my father every word of the movie, *The Adventures of Milo and Otis*—all 85 minutes of Dudley Moore's narration about the lovable adventures of "the curious cat and pug nose pup." Delighted, my father in turn recited Kipling's entire epic poem, *Gunga Din*, especially savoring the final lines: "Tho' I've belted you and flayed you. By the livin' Gawd that made you. You're a better man than I am, Gunga Din!"

"I think maybe Grandpa had Asperger's," Benjy said.

"Maybe," I said. "He's part of your male line, just like me."

"Did you ride the short bus to school?"

"No, I never did."

"Did you get bullied on the long bus?"

"Sometimes. Some people thought I was different, I'm sure."

"You weren't 'normal,' but you weren't too different."

"That sounds about right," I said, grinning.

"I'm glad I'm not normal," Benjy declared. "Normal is boring. I like being different."

"I like you being different, too," I said. In truth, there had been times when I had wished Benjy had been less different, that he would shoot baskets with me, or help me fix things around the house, or listen intently as I taught him how to drive a car—all the quality-time things I'd done with my father. Annie was usually able to get me through those mourning spells, and I hadn't felt one in years. But now I felt one tapping me on the shoulder. Maybe, I thought, there was quality-time thing we could share an interest in right here on my computer monitor?

"So this old car Grandpa had when I was growing up was called a

Corvair," I explained, hoping to pique his interest. "It was a very different car, built way back in the Sixties. And now I'm curious about it. I'm
actually fantasizing about getting one, maybe."

"We have a car, Dad," Benjy pointed out. "A Toyota Camry."

True. In a weirdly ironic twist, I owned an ultra-competent, ultra-
boring Toyota Camry, the very car with such serious safety issues that
many commentators were now comparing it to the unsafe-at-any-speed
Corvair. In fact, my Camry's recall notice had just arrived in the mail.

"Grandpa loved his Corvairs. We had really good times in it. Maybe,
if I got one, you and I could have good times in it together?"

"It's an old car, Dad," Benjy pointed out. "Really old."

"You're right," I admitted. "But I've been thinking I'd like a hobby.
I'd work on the car for fun. Maybe we could work on it together?"

"I don't know anything about cars, Dad. Neither do you."

"But I do know something about cars," I protested, "I worked at a
service station after school when I was your age." Which was true as far
as it went, but I didn't do much more than pump gas and check oil in
the days before all the stations went self-serve. I basically knew enough
about cars to know I didn't know much. But everything I'd read said the
Corvair was an easy car to work on and parts were plentiful. There were
even Corvair clubs across the country full of real experts who helped their
fellow Corvair owners out if they hit a snag. "If you leave home, I'll have
a lot of time on my hands. A hobby would keep me off the streets."

"You don't live on the streets," Benjy said. "We have a house."

"It's a figure of speech," I explained. "I'd have something fun to do
while I'm alone."

Even with the explanation, Benjy eyed me curiously. Usually, he was
the one who had the obsession that I then tried to defuse with common
sense. Now the tables were turned. "You should keep up the gardens
like Mom did," he finally said. "Everything's dying."

Two years after Annie's sudden passing, Benjy rarely spoke of her
or betrayed any emotion over her death, so I wanted to encourage the
discussion. "That's a good idea. Maybe we could keep up her garden together?" I suggested, even though I disliked gardening. "We could eat
fresh vegetables again."

"No, thank you," Benjy said firmly. "Neither of us even likes fresh vegetables. Besides, Mom didn't make me work in the garden because I don't like to put my hands in dirt. It feels weird. And once I saw a lizard. I hate lizards."

"But now, as a memory of her, maybe we ought to? That would make Mom happy, wouldn't it?"

"That doesn't make sense, Dad," Benjy said, his only emotion being annoyance. "Mom is dead. She can't be happy if she's dead. And why would she be happy to see me do something she didn't make me do when she was alive because she knew I didn't like it?"

He was right. It didn't make sense. It looked like we wouldn't be gardening together. Or talking any more today about Annie.

"So I guess for a hobby if we're not going to grow fresh vegetables, we're stuck with a Corvair," I said.

"That doesn't make sense either, Dad," Benjy said. "It's just an old car."

"I know. That's the point. It's old. It would be fun. Old is fun."

"Old is not fun. It's just old," Benjy insisted.

"I'm just curious about Corvairs, okay?" I said, trying not to sound as annoyed as he did.

"It's just an old car, Dad," he repeated several more times. Then he went up to his room, satisfied that his common sense had won the day over my nonsensical obsession. And he was right.

But tomorrow was a different story.

CHAPTER 3

"But it's just an old car, Dad!" Benjy scolded, his disapproval loud and clear despite the usual flat tone of his voice. It was three days later, he had just come home from school, the envelope from Wheeler hadn't arrived, and I'd just informed him that an hour earlier I'd bought a Corvair in an eBay auction. "You always tell me to control myself and not act impulsively," Benjy protested. "Why didn't you control yourself and not act impulsively?"

"It wasn't totally impulsive," I muttered meekly, shifting uncomfortably in my chair. "I did a lot of intensive research."

"It was as impulsive as anything I do," he fumed. "You acted obsessively and compulsively."

"All right, all right, I'm guilty," I admitted, crumbling under Benjy's withering cross-examination. "It was too perfect to pass up and I'm not perfect. In my defense, I will say that I put in a ridiculously low bid, so I think I got a good deal. Here, let me show you." I motioned to Benjy to sit beside me at my computer.

"I don't need to see it," he resisted. "It's just an old car."

"Come on, it's interesting."

"I doubt it," he grumbled, finally sitting down.

On my computer monitor, I pulled up a Craigslist ad for a 1965 Corvair convertible with an automatic transmission. "Listen to this," I said, reading: "'If rust is your thing, this is your car. The floors have more holes than Swiss cheese. Motor sounds angry and leaks oil. Tetanus shot recommended. First $500 takes it.'"

Benjy drew a blank, so I explained. "He's joking about how awful

the car is that he's trying to sell. Swiss cheese is full of holes. It's a joke."
Benjy still didn't laugh. His humor worked a different, more literal way.
Sarcasm, insincerity, puns, and word play were not his thing.

"I don't think that sounds like a good deal," he said.

"You're absolutely right. Which is why that's not the car I bought.
I'm just explaining why I thought the one I did buy was a good deal." I
pulled up the eBay auction page for my newly acquired 1965 Corvair
convertible. "See? It's the very same model, it runs great, has only a tiny
bit of rust so no tetanus shots are required. The seller claims it doesn't
leak oil—even though every Corvair leaks or burns oil—and the motor
sounds friendly. It wasn't all that much more expensive. Plus!" I raised
my voice for the boffo finale. "It's the very same year and model Corvair
that Grandpa had, that we rode around in when I was a boy. Except
Grandpa had a four door and I wanted a convertible. He'll forgive me,
I'm sure. Isn't that neat? That we now own this car?"

But Benjy didn't share my excitement. "You always yell at me to not
be obsessive."

"I don't yell at you. That's an exaggeration. Look, I spent nearly
ninety minutes talking to the seller. He's the President of the Florida
Corvair Club. He rebuilt the engine, transmission, brakes, all the mechanical systems in the car. He installed modern front seats with head
rests and shoulder harnesses, because cars in the Sixties didn't have those
safety features. He swore the car was in great shape. So I made a ridiculously low bid and won. Let's celebrate. We'll have a blast."

Benjy didn't feel a celebratory blast coming on. "What if I want to
get a car?" he asked. "You'll take up both spaces in the garage."

"Benjy, you decided not to get a driver's license," I pointed out. "If
you don't have a license, you can't have a car."

"They won't let me drive because of my Asperger's," he complained,
as he often did when the subject of his driving a car came up. "They
discriminate against people who they consider disabled! We're not disabled, we're just different."

"Benjy," I corrected, "I don't think you're being fair. The DMV re-
quires that you get a medical evaluation from the doctor and pass a special driving exam because of your Asperger's. That's very different from

saying they won't let you drive. We've talked about this many times." In fact, we'd talked about it many, many, many, many times.

"You didn't have to get a special medical evaluation to drive."

"No."

"So it's discrimination. I think it violates the Americans with Disabilities Act. Which is the Law of the Land since 1990, thanks to the efforts of Justin Dart and other people with differences." Stricken by polio as a youth, Dart was denied an opportunity to become a school-teacher because he was confined to a wheelchair; he then dedicated his life to fighting for equal rights and access for persons with disabilities. He was one of Benjy's heroes.

"They have to think of the safety of everyone on the road. It seems fair to me." I wasn't wild about any teenage boys driving on the road, let alone my only son who often had trouble staying focused on the task at hand.

Fortunately, he changed the subject. Unfortunately, he changed it back to the absurdity of my Corvair purchase. "This car is in Fort Lauderdale, Florida," he announced. "Fort Lauderdale, Florida is on the southeast coast of Florida, farther away than Disney World. Disney World is 826 miles from our house." Benjy liked to pore over maps, and we had driven to Disney World many years earlier; that particular mileage factoid had stuck in his mind.

"It's about a thousand miles," I admitted. "The seller said I could drive the car home, no problem. So, with your spring break coming up, I thought we'd fly down there and take a few days to drive it home. Maybe even stop at Disney World again. Whaddya say?"

Benjy put the kibosh on that idea. "I can't leave home. The letter from Wheeler might come."

"Benjy, Wheeler said the letter wouldn't come for another month. You were there when the head of the Asperger's Program said that."

"It might come," he insisted. "I can stay here by myself while you get the car."

I sighed. Benjy desperately wanted to live on his own; it was a point of pride for him as a "different but not disabled" person. But without someone around to remind Benjy of the daily necessities of life, such as taking a shower or his meds when he was supposed to, those necessities often didn't get done. That was why Wheeler was such a good fit for him; in addition to giving Benjy an excellent college education, their special Asperger's program would help him achieve his dream of living independently.

"If I can go away to college by myself, why can't I stay at home by myself?" he asked. He fixed his big brown eyes on me in a determined gaze to drive his point home. "I can live by myself, Dad," he declared. "I'm nineteen years old. I'm practically an adult."

He had a point. In his own home, where he already had detailed checklists and schedules that he followed every day, he probably could live by himself for a few days. And if there was a problem, Mavis could come over. She was always volunteering to do that; she'd done it while I'd stayed with Annie at the hospital. So why not?

I knew very well why not. Because ever since I had become a single parent, I had worried myself to a frazzle about everything having to do with Benjy. I was overprotective to a fault. With Annie gone, nothing bad would happen to our son. I wasn't letting her down. Not on my watch!

Still, he was right. His logic was impeccable. He was growing up; maybe it was time to loosen up? Annie would say he could do it; she always saw the positive. "Let him try," she would say. "Let him stretch. Better to have tried and failed than never to have tried at all." Why couldn't I think that way? He had his checklists. He was a responsible kid—more responsible than most—even if he did have Asperger's. Perhaps he was more responsible because of his Asperger's. He wouldn't hold a wild party or trash the house like a lot of other kids might. He'd just follow his regular weekend routines: play his NASCAR video game, watch movies and TV, read a book, and do his homework. And it would be great, everything would be fine, he'd love it, and it would boost his confidence in himself and his life skills before he went off to Wheeler. He would stretch. It would be a positive learning experience. Everything would be fine.

On the first Saturday after the end of my triumphant eBay auction, I flew to Florida to claim my prize. I estimated it would take three days for me to drive the Corvair the thousand miles home, assuming one or two breakdowns, which I considered inevitable. Benjy hoped it would take longer; I'd overloaded the fridge with his favorite chicken tenders, apples, and bottled water. *National Treasure* and all his other favorite DVDs were ready to go. He was itching to deliver Denny Hamlin another crushing defeat on the NASCAR racetrack. He was so excited that he had even agreed, grudgingly, to my insistence that Mavis stop in and check on him once a day. "It's not negotiable, Benjy," I said as I prepped the Mother of All Lists for him to complete each day I was gone.

"I'm about to go away to college, Dad!" he protested, feeling insulted. "I've lived by myself before! I know how! I don't need help!"

"Benjy, those were summer camps and programs where you had an adult counselor. We do this my way or I don't go. I'll get the car shipped here instead. Besides, staffers at Wheeler will do the same checking up on you when you're there, so you might as well get used to it."

"Dad, some travel experts recommend that you check in for a domestic flight two hours or more before its scheduled departure," he then informed me, practically shoving me out the door.

I made my flight, needless to say. Now, in the spring steam bath of Fort Lauderdale, I exited the airport terminal along with hordes of spring breakers around Benjy's age. Their bacchanalia had already begun; many of the teens were sloppily drunk, yanking down each other's shorts and lighting up cigarettes. Watching these "normal" kids behave badly annoyed me, until they reminded me of what a terrific child I had left behind at home, and how blessed I was to have him. When I was mired in the daily challenges of raising Benjy, I sometimes forgot that. I was grateful to these kids for helping me remember.

Wally Krawchek, my Corvair's seller, was not difficult to spot among the rowdy teens; his white hair and deep tan helped identify him, but he was also the only person in the terminal with a shirt, hat, and folded umbrella all adorned with Corvairs. "They're callin' for afternoon thunderstorms," he explained about the umbrella after we'd warmly greeted each other. "I don't usually drive a Corvair when they predict rain, and they predict afternoon thunderstorms all the time, so that's why yours has low miles." We strolled to the parking garage elevator and he pushed the button. "Not driving in the rain—that's also why your car has minimal rust. As you'll see, I'm a stickler for accuracy in my auction descriptions."

"No worries," I assured him. "I know it's just as you described. You had me at president of the Florida Corvair Club. That's exactly what I needed to hear. I'm sure you did a wonderful job restoring it." There were only a few wispy clouds: no rain today. Perfect driving weather.

"I take the CORSA creed and my oath of office seriously," he stressed, extremely seriously. "I promote the Corvair hobby and recruit new people to it. I take Corvairs to car shows, educate people on the car, and personally do as much as I can to get Corvairs back on the road. I have refreshed nine Corvairs so far—sold six and still have three I'm working on. So what I think we got here is the perfect match of the buyer who is new to the Corvair hobby and the Corvair that will keep him in the hobby." He grinned, pleased.

After the elevator came and we entered, Wally pushed the button for the top level. He was taller and thinner than me, yet had short, thick fingers, with grease in the ridges of his calluses. From working on cars, I guessed. He hadn't looked me in the eye yet. He was a retired engineer, which made sense; he seemed more comfortable with machines than with people.

"Just so there's no misunderstanding," he continued, still very serious, "you used the term 'restore.' I did not 'restore' the car. I 'refreshed' it. There is an important difference. I refreshed all the mechanicals. You'll have to restore the paint and body work. I believe I was clear on that in the auction."

"Yes, you were, and I understand," I assured him. "I didn't mean to imply that I was expecting a fully restored car. I was sloppy in my language and didn't use the correct term. Sorry."

"That's fine. Now that you're a member of the Corvair Brotherhood, you'll learn it all soon enough." He smiled, but still didn't look me in the eye.

I liked the sound of "Corvair Brotherhood." Like I had been inducted into a secret society.

"Got the repair manuals?" he asked as the elevator slowed.

I confessed that I didn't have them yet.

"It's a forty-five-year-old car. You'll need those manuals. You work on cars much?"

I confessed that I didn't work on cars much.

"You will now." He smiled for the first time. "It's a forty-five-year-old car," he repeated.

The elevator doors opened and we stepped out onto the roof deck. Which was empty—save for one vehicle.

My new Corvair shimmered in the hot Florida sun. Jet black with its white convertible top up, the reflection off its polished chrome three-bar wire wheel covers was blinding. I grinned like a Cheshire cat.

"Well?" Wally prodded. "What do you think?"

My grin became a giggle. "Your photos didn't do it justice. It's gorgeous."

He looked down at his shoes and chuckled, pleased. "I always thought it was gorgeous, too," he admitted. "Didn't want to oversell it, though. Couldn't sleep at night if I did."

Of course, as the car's new owner, I was highly prejudiced. But even objective critics loved GM's exterior redesign of the Corvair for the 1965 model year—what became known as the "Late Model" Corvair. In my Google search, I uncovered *Car and Driver* magazine's eminent writer David E. Davis gushing:

[T]he Corvair is — in our opinion — the most important new car of the entire crop of '65 models, and the most beautiful car to appear in this country since before World War II.... When the pictures of the '65 Corvair arrived in our offices, the man who opened the envelope actually let out a great shout of delight and amazement on first seeing the car, and in thirty seconds the whole staff was charging around, each wanting to be the first to show somebody else, each wanting the vicarious kick of hearing that characteristic war-whoop from the first-time viewer.

Two score and five years later, I knew just how that guy in the *Car and Driver* office felt. The Late Model design had not lost its looks. I could still see, as GM's seductive ads purred, the "shape that blends elegance with excitement." The exterior's gently rounded fenders, bisected by crisp lines, inspired by Raymond Loewy's famed design of the classic Coke bottle, would even at its advanced age win any beauty pageant over nearly all of today's cookie-cutter cars, including my boring Camry. Black, white, chrome—to me, this Corvair was an Art Deco sculpture on wheels. I understood now how my father had fallen in love with his Late Model back in the day—I was falling in love myself.

I inspected the car's surface for flaws and found all the rust spots, dings, faded paint, and road rash that Wally's photos had revealed, but no surprises. I opened the rear hatch; the engine looked as if it had just been installed on the assembly line. The interior wasn't quite that fresh, but still did not disappoint. The modern front seats had headrests and integrated shoulder and lap belts, with no rips or tears in the cloth. The carpet was new. The chrome window frames and horn button were pitted from aging, hardly a major issue.

On the flight down, I had braced myself for disappointment. Instead, I found myself over the moon, and moved by this encounter with a man of such high honor who refused to oversell his beloved car. Why couldn't life always be so satisfying?

"Ready to take her for a spin?" Wally asked.

"Should we do the paperwork first? Signing over the title and all?"

Wally eyed me with suspicion. "Don't you want to drive it first? Make sure you're satisfied?" I saw a thought cross his face: How could this guy not want to drive the car before he signs on the dotted line? Was I part of some elaborate scam that he needed to run from this instant?

"Before I drive it," I warned Wally, "I have a confession to make."

He looked stricken, fixing his gaze on me at last. His Scam Alert was flashing Bright Red. "You don't have the money?" he asked. "You changed your mind?"

"No, no. It's just that I've never driven a Corvair on the open road. Only in an empty parking lot. With my learner's permit, and my father teaching me to drive."

"Really?" Wally exploded in relief. "Seriously?" Scam Alert reduced to Yellow.

"And I've only ridden in two of them." I told him about Dad's Corvairs.

"Pity that some people go through life driving nothing but ordinary cars." He tossed me the keys. "You're about to have all kinds of fun."

"Before we go, I should call my son. Tell him I arrived, check in on him." Wally gestured for me to go ahead. As I dialed my cell phone, he kneeled down to stalk dust that had dared come to rest on the Vair's black paint.

Benjy answered just before the answering machine picked up. "HELLO!" he bellowed.

"Benjy, it's Dad. I'm in Florida. I made it to the airport in plenty of time."

"Okay."

"How are you?"

"Fine."

"Did you make lunch?"

"Yes."

"What?"

"The usual. Chicken tenders."

"Take your afternoon meds?"

"Yes."

"Okay. Well, I'm standing beside our new Corvair, and it's gorgeous." Wally beamed at this. "I hope you'll like it cuz I sure do. I think we'll have a lot of fun in it."

"It's just an old car, Dad," said Benjy, not bothering to hide his disdain.

"It's not old," I corrected. "It's classic."

"It's old, Dad," he corrected right back. "Old is not classic." Always the Truth Teller.

I sighed. "So. Anything else?"

"No."

"Okay. Well, I'll sign off so I can start driving home. If nothing goes wrong, I should be home Monday night or Tuesday. Is that still okay?"

"Okay."

I heard a boozy chant well up from the teenage revelers over at the terminal impatiently waiting for their hotel bus. "Benjy," I said into the phone, "you are a really, really great kid, and I'm proud of you. I don't tell you that often enough. I'll call you in a few hours, okay?"

He said nothing, then asked, "Dad?"

"Yes, Benjy."

"The letter from Wheeler?"

"It'll come in a few more weeks."

"It came today."

Hearing Benjy's voice, my heart sank and my knees buckled. I winced hard, as if that would make the bad news go away.

"It wasn't all we had hoped for," Benjy said flatly, yet with a disappointment that was deafening.

"Benjy, it's okay," I told him, even though I knew it wasn't. How could I be a thousand miles away from him at a time like this? What kind of father was I, anyway?

"I didn't get in," he said, his voice cracking. Benjy usually didn't display much emotion, but when he did cry, it was a wounded howl. Even Wally heard it; when he saw the pain in my face, he took a few steps away to give me privacy.

"Benjy, Wheeler is not the only college...."

"It *is* the only college for me, Dad!" he wailed.

"This is going to be all right, Benjy. I mean that. And I'm going to get there as soon as I can, okay?" He didn't respond, so I repeated. "Okay? Benjy? You there?"

"There's no place for me," he said softly. "No place anywhere."

"There is a place for you and we will find it, Benjy," I told him, trying to hold back my own tears. "I've never been surer of anything in my life."

Benjy was silent. Finally, he said, "I'm too different." His wailing erupted again, louder this time.

As I tried to calm Benjy down, I kicked the driver's side front tire of the Corvair again and again and again, violently scuffing the tire polish Wally had so meticulously applied. He looked over, but I waved him away.

Why was I here buying this lousy Deathmobile? What was I thinking? I couldn't stand to look at it. I didn't want it anymore.

I needed to get home. Now.

CHAPTER 4

After I explained what happened to Wally, he offered to cancel our deal. He said he could try to sell the car to someone else, and if it was for a lower price, I could make up the difference. He was being more than fair.

With the spring sun now in full retreat, I called the airlines. But spring break meant everything was booked going into or out of all the nearby airports until at least Monday, two days away. "Maybe there's a bus from here, or a train?" I wondered aloud to Wally. "Or I could rent a car here and just drive the wheels off it until I get home."

"Why rent a car when you just bought one?" Wally asked. "You'll be home in time for lunch tomorrow if you drive all night."

With great skepticism, I first eyed Wally and then the Corvair. "This car? You think this car will make it a thousand miles in less than one full day?"

"I can't guarantee it," he said. "I couldn't guarantee a rented car either. But, heck, yes, I'd bet on this car over a rental car. This car will make it." He fished in the Corvair's glove box and found a booklet. "And if it breaks down, this is the CORSA membership roster. You call me any hour of the night. At dawn, I'll call the CORSA member nearest to you. If he can't help you, I'll call the next one. You may have to wait a few hours. But you will get help if you need it."

He eyed me proudly. Still, I was skeptical. Very skeptical. "In June," he went on, "I'm driving my '69 Vair fourteen hundred miles to the CORSA annual convention. There's a bunch of us caravanning from

Florida. We do it every year. Most every car makes it, and if one does break down we fix it and keep going. It's no big thing."

"But you know how to fix these," I protested. "You carry parts and tools. I worked in a service station once, but I only pumped gas. I know which end of the hammer hits the nail, but that's about it." I walked around the car, shaking my head. "I was going to take three days at least. I figured two breakdowns—minimum."

Wally raised himself up, squinted his eyes, and fixed me with a glare. Clearly, I'd wounded his pride. "You're falling into the popular misconception that Corvairs are defective, unsafe junk. That's bull. That's an unusual way to start your Corvair hobby. I strongly suggest that you forget what you think you know about this car, about it being a piece of junk or a killer car. It's just not so."

"All right," I said. "I am opening my mind."

Wally looked around the roof; we were the only two people in sight. He lowered his voice anyway. "Look," he confided. "This is too much information, maybe, but I'm queerer than a three dollar bill, see, not that I go out of my way to advertise it. But most everybody in the Corvair club knows it and they still elected me President of the Corvair Club of Florida. Which may be a big joke to most people, but really is a big honor in the Corvair world, okay? And you know why they did that? Cuz Corvair people got an open mind. They have to, because this car is different from every other boring car on the road. Ed Cole, the engineer who designed the Corvair, he opened his mind and completely re-imagined the small car. This is a unique car, maybe the most innovative American car of the past fifty years. Sure, it has quirks and flaws, like any new technology, and they cut some corners to save some money because they had to design most everything from scratch, and it'll never win a drag race against a big fat V-8. But Nader was wrong; when government and university scientists studied the Corvair forwards and back, they found it as safe as or safer than comparable cars. It got a bum rap that it never recovered from, and no one knows or cares. It's reliable and safe and cheap to operate and a lot of the people I've met in one are pretty darn special. They love it because it's different. And so do I." His eyes welled up.

"I really appreciate you telling me that," I said, "and I'm sorry if I offended you. I have a very different son, believe me, so I love different. And right now, he's in the middle of a crisis at home, I need to get back as soon as I can, and this is a very old car. That's all I meant to say."

He nodded, pulled a kerchief from his pocket, wiped his eyes, and continued. "If you're worried cuz it won't be reliable, well, the mechanicals are new. I vouch for the mechanicals. You can rely on them to get you home. However, if you are worried cuz the car's different, then the Corvair is not the right car for you, and you are not the right owner for the Corvair. So here's your chance, you're free to back out. Even though we got a binding deal under eBay rules, I not only won't force you to take it, I flat out won't let you take it. This Vair's next owner will respect it and honor its differences. In turn, it will respect him."

Two hours later, the last glimmer of the day's light dried up as I raced my new Corvair up the Atlantic coast of Florida. Originally, to not tax the car too much, I'd planned to take it home at a leisurely pace along the scenic coastal highway. That plan was now toast. My new plan was to drive the ever-living-stuffing out of this car along traffic-choked Interstate 95 until the Corvair either pulled into my driveway or blew up.

Before Wally finally signed over the car's title to me, I had to persuade him that, Cross My Heart and Hope to Die, I truly was not a closed-minded Corvair-hater unable to embrace the car's uniqueness—that, indeed, as a newly inducted member of the Corvair Brotherhood, I positively celebrated its differences and would do my utmost to uphold the CORSA creed. His words and passion for the Corvair inspired me as I left the terminal's parking garage; I noticed and appreciated the car's heavy rear end as it securely planted itself into the tight curves of the labyrinth of airport exit roads. The steering was light as a feather, even without the power assist that almost every modern car has. The high-pitched ringing of the aluminum air-cooled engine delighted me; it was the same whine my father's Corvair had made as it assaulted the steep hill I grew up on. It was indeed a very different car. And I loved it.

But then I merged onto I-95, which ran right beside the airport. As I reached highway cruising speed, my eager elopement with this car suddenly seemed headed for an even more eager annulment. The interior of the Corvair was now the vortex of a Force Five tornado. Not being part of the car's mechanical refresh, the original rubber weather seals around the windows, doors, and convertible roof had dried up; chunks of decades-old rubber were blowing away before my eyes, and, at times, into my eyes. The howling wind combined with the rattling doors and bouncing roof in a deafening conspiracy to break my will to drive on.

After an hour in this audiological torture chamber, chugging along in the right lane, the lone driver actually obeying the speed limit, battling truckers who sprinted up to my rear bumper to get me to go faster or get the heck off their highway, I forgot Wally's Ode to the Misunderstood Corvair and conceived a plot to abandon the car. Hopefully, once my new Corvair broke down, as it surely would, it would do so near an open rental car counter, a bus station, or a promising place to hitchhike. I would then resume my journey home, Corvair-less, and let Wally know where he could reclaim the car's lifeless remains, apologizing to him that I'd discovered I really wasn't Corvair material after all.

Suddenly, I leaped from my driver's seat as if a cobra had slithered into my lap. It was my cell phone; I'd put it between my thighs and set it to vibrate because there was no way I could hear it ring. The Caller I.D. said it was my house calling, which meant Mavis, as Benjy rarely called anyone. I'd told her the bad news about Wheeler before I pulled out of the airport, and asked her to check on Benjy. She was now at our house, bless her. I cut my speed so I could hear her.

"HELLO!" I shouted.

"He climbed into bed, pulled the covers over his head, and told me to go away," I thought I heard Mavis say.

"Did he take his meds before he went to bed?" I hollered. "Eat anything?"

"YES!" she shouted back. "Where are you? It's so loud!"

I explained why I sounded like I was speaking from the inside of a jet engine. "Was he still upset?" I asked, as I struggled to deal with an annoyed truck driver who flashed his lights at me to move over when there was no place to move over to.

She said Benjy seemed calm, and thought he had fallen asleep, which was the best possible news. She offered to spend the night at our house, but from her description of things, we agreed it wasn't necessary. The trucker honked an enraged symphony on his air horns as he passed me.

Two hours later, near Daytona Beach, with the gas gauge just above Empty, I eased the Corvair off the highway and found a gas station. With my ears ringing as if I'd been in the front row at a rock concert, I filled up with Premium grade, per Wally's orders, because anything else would make the engine knock. Another middle-aged driver squeegeed the windshield of his newish Mustang at the pump beside me. "Hey, great car," he purred, walking around and inspecting it with greater care than I had just a couple hours earlier. "What year is it?"

I told him, along with a few added details. With the sun now down, the cooler outside air made me shiver. Suddenly, I needed to find a bathroom. Real suddenly.

"I had one of those," the Mustang driver reminisced. "Loved it. Handled beautifully. Great for a teenager. Easy on the gas, easy to fix. Nader killed it, though. Ya never see 'em anymore."

I shifted my weight from side to side. The Mustang Man looked ready to talk about the car all night. "I don't mean to be impolite, but I really need to get inside," I said.

He knew what I meant. "When you're our age," he winked, not bothering to finish the thought. "You got a great car there. Enjoy."

Inside the station's convenience store, after I no longer had to hop around on one foot, I bought a prefab sub sandwich, a six-pack of energy drinks, a case of hyper-caffeinated sodas, and industrial-strength earplugs.

"Had it long?" the manager at the cash register asked, nodding toward the Corvair.

I checked my watch. "About four hours," I told him. "Bought it on eBay and just picked it up in Fort Lauderdale."

"Get a lot of stops here from people pickin' up cars they bought on eBay," the manager informed me dourly. "They think havin' no road salt to rust 'em down here is a big deal. Turns out most of 'em are disappointed."

I was suddenly very eager to hit the road.

"In fact, I had one guy turn around and head back south," the manager droned on as I jammed my new industrial-strength earplugs deep into my auditory canals. "Said he was gonna beat the living…" I grinned and waved as I went out the door, pretending I couldn't hear him.

"That boy of yours is amazing!" I heard my father exclaim as the highway miles piled up and my mind wandered. Dad and I had parked outside the bathroom door, eavesdropping on Benjy, who was in the tub with Annie, booming out a story about Thomas the Tank Engine and his friends on the Island of Sodor. He had not stumbled over a single word. "I've never heard a boy his age read so beautifully!" Dad raved.

"He's not reading," I told Dad. At the time, Benjy was not yet three years old.

My father's jaw dropped. "He's a genius," he said softly. "My grandson is a genius."

With traffic thinning as truckers called it a night, paper towels stuffed where the rubber sound insulation had rotted away and my earplugs sealing off my bruised ear drums, I could finally hear the thoughts and memories that this old car stirred. Naturally, in a Corvair so much like my father's, the first memories that came were of him.

Not long after Dad and I listened to Benjy in the bath, while I was away from home on business, Annie called me late at night to report that Dad had just phoned. This was odd. My father was always an early-to-bed, early-to-rise guy; at the time he called, he usually would have been sound asleep for hours.

"He was so absolutely insistent," Annie said, her concern evident. "He insisted Benjy had to go to Dartmouth College, and we had to apply there immediately."

At the time, Benjy was still a month shy of his third birthday.

"At first I thought he was joking," she continued. "But he was dead serious and absolutely obsessive about it. It was very strange. Something's wrong."

I waited till morning to phone Dad at his retirement community. I thought a good night's sleep might clear up his odd behavior.

I was wrong.

"Benjy must go to Dartmouth," Dad insisted moments after he answered. "He's a special boy, a genius. Dartmouth is the only place for him."

"Dad," I ventured gently, trying to be oh-so-careful in my choice of words so as not to offend my father, a very proud Dartmouth alumnus who may have never forgiven me for not following him there. "There's plenty of time for Benjy to grow up and let his talents fully develop before he decides where he should go to college. After all, he hasn't even turned three."

There was a long pause. A very long pause. I realized that Dad had lost track of how young his grandson really was.

I soon learned from my father's doctor that dementia was destroying his prodigious mind and memory. There was little anyone could do about the disease's advance. Fortunately, his retirement community was well versed in the challenges of caring for a resident with dementia and pledged that Dad would be safe, secure, and comfortable.

Another memory, from a year later: As I waited in line to pick up Benjy from preschool, the Headmistress called me into her office for a private chat. "Your son is unique," she told me.

I beamed proudly. "All children are, aren't they?" I answered, trying to appear modest.

"In thirty-five years, I've never seen another child quite like him," she said, treading ever so cautiously, in the same way that I had in speaking to my father about Dartmouth. Of course, I knew that Benjy was different from the other kids. I just didn't realize that difference had a name. The headmistress urged me to take Benjy to a child psychiatrist, who ultimately diagnosed Asperger's Syndrome.

"He's different, that's all," Annie said as I stared into space, cursing my genes, after we'd left the doctor's office. "Maybe there won't be sports, but there will be other things." And there were—we read books and watched movies together, and had long debates over them. But not knowing those things were in our future, I was in shock.

And if I was in shock, Annie and I realized my father's reaction would be even worse. By then, Dad had moved into our home; the retirement community could no longer handle him. And we were having a tough time coping. His behavior was increasingly erratic; he'd frequently erupt in anger, or dissolve into tears, seemingly over nothing. His wise and sober judgment had given way to confusion. Suddenly, his mail contained hundreds of magazines he'd never read, cheeses of the month he'd never eat, and deeds for timeshares in places he'd never visit. After his death, we discovered that, sight unseen, he had paid an astronomical amount of money for a family burial plot in a cemetery somewhere in West Virginia that had sent him a glossy brochure. The salesman refused to undo the deal when I confronted him about taking advantage of my father's mental incapacity. "Y'know," Annie comforted me, looking around the place, "of course he got ripped off, but it's not that bad. It's peaceful, with the mountain view and everything. I like it. Maybe he knew what he was doing?" So I swallowed my pride, and buried Dad there. And then, two years ago, I placed Annie beside him.

In the end, we never did tell Dad the news about Benjy's diagnosis. Dementia had too great a grip on him. Why burden him with news of Benjy's occupational therapy, psychological therapy, physical therapy, tests, expert evaluations, reevaluations, and day after day of "floor time" designed to teach Benjy how to socialize with others? Why trouble him over our never-ending struggles with health insurers and the public school system? Or the fights between Annie and me over the crushing cost of providing Benjy with his own personal "shadow" in his private school classroom so he would stay on task and not disrupt other students, or the weird fad diets that may have helped an Asperger's child someplace that we then felt compelled to try? And on and on? Why tell him that he and I, thanks to our genes, may have helped make Benjy so different from other children? I knew how hard I was taking the thought of my culpability; I could only imagine how devastated he would be. I thought it might kill him.

So, for the next year, my father and my son played gleefully together on our living room floor, reciting stories and poetry to each other for hours on end. And Dad told Benjy, again and again, that one day he would go to a school where he would learn even more wonderful stories that he could read and recite, just as Dad had when he was growing up.

It was a magical school, like a Hogwarts, but it was real and it taught only Muggles; it was a place for geniuses called Dartmouth College, and it was the only college on earth for him.

CHAPTER 5

With the eastern horizon offering up dawn's first light, the Corvair passed South of the Border at the boundary between the Carolinas, the legendary faux Mexican food/gas/smokes/fireworks/trinkets palace; for the past hundred miles, billboards had blared come-ons like *You Never Sausage a Place! You're Always a Weiner at Pedro's!*

I'd driven all night, save for the one gas stop. With the roar of the Corvair finally blocked from my ear drums, I was warming to it again. It hadn't broken down yet, which was a major plus. In fact, the car's refreshed engine and transmission had performed flawlessly, as Wally had promised, cruising more than seven hundred miles without so much as a hiccup, while achieving 23 mpg—dynamite gas mileage from a car built in the days when gas mileage was often measured in single digits. As truck after impatient truck passed me while I stubbornly stuck to the speed limit, the car held its line, stable in their turbulent wake.

Now, the Vair and I were both running on empty and needed to stop, and it would be far better for both of us if that stop was voluntary. Then I was jolted wide awake by a sign for "Wheeler College—Next Exit." My route had returned me to the Scene of the Crime against my son.

As I pumped high-test gas at the same station Benjy and I had used when we last visited the school, I mused wacked-out, sleep-deprived thoughts about rousing the dean of Wheeler from his bed to demand that he immediately make right the horrible injustice his underlings had perpetrated against my son. I'm ashamed to say it took me far more than just a moment to dismiss this idea and realize that it would be vindictive and juvenile, not to mention counterproductive. Perhaps Benjy would want to transfer here one day. Better not to burn any bridges. With a fresh six-pack of energy drinks beside me, I turned tail instead, and retreated back to the interstate, patting myself on the back for so magnanimously turning the other cheek.

Still, I couldn't help but wonder why Wheeler had rejected Benjy. He was Honor Roll at his high school. He had fine test scores. He had recommendations from the state's most prestigious special education officials. His extra-curriculars were excellent. His application was top-notch.

I recalled the day of Benjy's final interview. He looked every inch the college man, wearing a blazer and tie for one of the few times in his life. Standing in the center of the school quadrangle near the statue of Ezekiel Wheeler, the philanthropic tobacco magnate who founded the school, soaking in the atmosphere of what he hoped would be his new home for the next four years, he proudly proclaimed, "There is a place for me. And I found it. Right here." To become one of just 10 students selected to attend the unique Asperger's program at Wheeler, he knew he had to impress the staffers who would interview him. He started pacing around like a prizefighter waiting for the bell to start round one, thinking about the answers he'd prepared to questions I'd suggested were likely to be asked.

"I was one of only twenty-five students with differences selected from my whole state to attend the Youth Leadership Forum last summer," Benjy answered when the two interviewers asked about his proudest achievement. "And it was a full scholarship, so my father didn't have to pay a thing!"

The staffers grinned, and so did I, even though I knew Benjy hadn't intended it as a joke.

"He's cheap," Benjy added, generating big laughs. This time, he grinned slyly. Now he was joking, which impressed the interviewers. Aspergians are often so literal that telling jokes is difficult.

"One of our projects was to go to the state capital and ask the legislators to declare October as 'Disability History and Awareness Month' in Virginia. And this year they did! I was very proud of that!"

Benjy was rolling. He told the interviewers he'd participated on panels at autism conferences, written articles about living with Asperger's for a special-education journal, written his own novel about the last superhero the world would ever see, and had already taken—and aced—college-level English and political science courses.

He wasn't just knocking the ball out of the park; he was belting it into another time zone.

But as the interview's first hour stretched into the second, Benjy yawned. This was no garden-variety yawn, small and easily stifled, but a loud, weary, bored, not-covering-the-mouth, dental-office-clean-and-floss-all-the-upper-and-lower-teeth-then-check-for-cavities yawn.

I hurriedly explained that we'd driven five hours from home to Wheeler that morning. If I could have covertly nudged Benjy under the table, I would have. But I couldn't get his attention.

The staffers smiled politely. One asked whether Benjy was prepared to live independently in a college setting. This is a big question facing many Aspergians hoping to attend college, and Benjy was no exception. Knowing the subject was sure to come up, I'd suggested Benjy rehearse some answers, and I sat back to watch him crush this fat pitch right down the middle of the strike zone.

"Sometimes I like to stay in bed and turn off the alarm and pull the covers up over my head," he admitted. "And sometimes I forget to take showers." Then came another mega-yawn.

The staffers smiled again, supportively, but I thought I read a different message as they looked to each other, as if saying, "This kid could require *a lot* of support from us. *Lots and lots* of support."

They asked Benjy if his first choice of college for the coming fall was Wheeler. It was another standard question we had prepared for.

"Actually," replied Benjy, "I wanted to go to Dartmouth College. But they don't have a special program for students with Asperger's. So I have to go to Wheeler."

I tried not to fall out of my chair, then told the staffers about my father's love of Dartmouth. They seemed to understand. I prayed Benjy would follow my lead, and try to explain his answer a bit, but he didn't.

The next thing we heard from Wheeler was the rejection letter.

After the interview, I asked Benjy why he had not given the answers we had practiced. Such as, "Sometimes I forget to take showers, but now I've put 'taking a shower' on my list of things to do before I go to bed." Not only did this answer showcase Benjy's strong desire to improve his independent living skills, it also happened to be true.

"Those were your answers," Benjy replied. "I answered my answers. I still do forget sometimes or I fall asleep early and don't do my list. That's the truth."

"But my answer was true, too!" I insisted. "Lots of people forget or fall asleep, that's no big deal. It came off sounding like a big deal. In an interview like that, you want to stress the positive, not the negative."

"Your answer wasn't as true as mine," he said. "I have Asperger's, Dad. That's why I'm applying for this program. This is the way I am. I can't help it."

At the end of our final interview, the Program Director said the school would not explain why an applicant was not selected; otherwise, the staff would be forever defending its difficult decisions to disappointed students and parents. So we will never know. But now, leaving Wheeler behind in the Corvair's rear-view mirror, I realized Benjy had been right and I had been wrong. His blunt honesty came from the heart—his heart. He wouldn't stoop to misleading the Wheeler interviewers by playing a character conjured up by his anxious father. He was proud of the real Benjy.

Five hours later, I eased the Corvair into our driveway, yanked up the parking brake, turned off the engine, and rested my forehead against the steering wheel. Stopping only for gas and bathroom breaks, my antique Art Deco sculpture had borne me a thousand miles in 17 hours. I didn't know if I would keep the car or not. But I'd always be grateful to it for safely bringing me home.

I unlocked the house and checked the TV room. This was Benjy's scheduled NASCAR video game time, but he wasn't there. I went up to his room and knocked softly. "Hey, dude, it's Dad," I announced.

"I'm asleep!" he claimed loudly, his voice muffled by layers of bed covers.

I went in anyway. At the head end of the bed, his quilt was pulled up over his head so that his size 13 feet stuck out before me. Often, I would tickle those feet, but not today. He wasn't in the mood, I was sure.

"Sleep okay?" I asked.

"Not really," he croaked. He sounded as if he hadn't slept a wink.

"You're not playing your game, huh?"

"No."

I sat on the bed beside him and scratched his back through the quilt. He loved back scratches. "Wanna talk about it?" I asked.

"No, thank you," he replied, emphatically.

"Maybe later, huh?"

"No, thank you!" More emphatically.

"Okay," I agreed. "I got the new car here. Drove it a thousand miles. Impressive, huh? For an old car?"

"Could you leave me alone, please? I'm going back to sleep."

Sleep sounded good. I called Wally to report my safe arrival. He said he told me so, and that I was now a true member of the Corvair Brotherhood. I hung up and then crashed onto my bed.

A few hours of sleep later, I returned to Benjy's room, and he again ordered me to leave. But this time, I had come armed with hot chicken tenders. "Time for lunch," I said as I poked my head into his room. "Late lunch or early dinner, your choice."

He scrambled up from his bed. His face was puffy from crying. He grabbed the tray and crunched into the biggest chicken tender.

"We knew the odds were against you," I said, sitting beside him on the bed, reviewing the Wheeler letter that he'd left on the kitchen table. "They had ten open slots and over two hundred applicants. And you were a finalist. They even invited you to apply again next year."

Benjy ate just one chicken tender before he dropped his head back on his pillow. "Do we have to talk about this now?" He yanked the quilt back over his head.

"Steven Spielberg, Warren Buffett, and Ted Turner," I pronounced, citing names Benjy recognized. "They were all turned down by their first choice of school." Under his plate of chicken tenders, I had placed a printout of an article on this very topic I had found online a few minutes earlier. "It wasn't the end for any of them, was it? Maybe it was more like a new beginning?"

He wasn't biting yet, so I re-baited my hook and kept trolling. "James Monroe Community College is an excellent school. And you've already got English and political science credits there from the dual enrollment courses you're taking. To go there for a year or two, get accustomed to the college workload and routine, then reapply to Wheeler—that could be the way to go."

Still no bite.

To get some kind of discussion started with him, I even tried to set him up for his favorite joke about my frugality. "We'd sure save a lot of money if you went to community college and lived at home."

No bite. Nothing.

"Are you sure there isn't anything you want to say or ask?" I prodded.

Benjy fired the covers off his head. "I want to leave home," he said firmly. "I'm nineteen years old. In a few months, I won't even be a teenager anymore. It's time for me to leave home and find my own place in the world."

"More and more young people are staying at home with their parents," I noted. "They're finding it can be a tough world out there, and that maybe home isn't so bad after all."

"I want to go," he said again. "If I have to stay here, it's like I'm disabled when I'm just different. If I make lists and stuff, I'll be okay. I just have to find a place that's right for me." With finality, he pulled the covers up over his head again.

"Benjy, if that's what you want, I will support you every way I possibly can. Okay?"

No reply.

"Listen," I said. "It's nice out and the sun's warm. Let's take a ride in the Corvair. We can put the top down and get some ice cream."

"No, thank you!" he blasted. "It's just an old car, Dad!"

I patted him under the covers. "We'll talk more later, okay?"

After I got up from his bed, he asked, "Dad, do you think my interview at Wheeler is why they rejected me?"

"I wondered about that on the drive up here. And you were right, you were absolutely right, and I was wrong. You showed them who you were, and that you knew you needed their help to live independently, and you were ready to learn from them. That was the right thing to do, the brave thing to do. I'm proud of you for doing it. And if that meant you weren't selected, then maybe that was never the right place for you. So now we will find the right place, okay?"

"There is no place," he said quietly. "I'm too different."

CHAPTER 6

The next morning, I gazed through the kitchen window and realized that Benjy was right about that Corvair now parked in our driveway. Yes, my father had loved Corvairs. And I was looking for a hobby—something to plug the gaping hole that Annie's passing and Benjy's leaving home for college would leave in my life. But, as Benjy said, and said, and said again, when you got right down to it, that thing in the driveway was still just an old car. It was not an answer to what ailed me, but an indulgence, and would likely become a time sink and a money pit. If I were an empty-nester, as I'd planned to be, perhaps I could justify it. But, with Benjy now staying in the nest and disdaining that old car every time we spoke about it, I feared it would push us apart. For three days, I'd been a Corvair owner. Now it was time to get rid of it.

Benjy rolled drowsily into the kitchen to take his meds. Still in his pajamas, his unruly long hair pushing out in every direction, he ignored me and was headed back to bed when he spotted the Corvair outside. "That's it?" he asked, accomplishing the difficult feat of sounding both incredulous and asleep.

"That's it," I affirmed. "So? What do you think?" I tried to keep him talking so he wouldn't retreat back under the covers.

"It's an old car, all right. Does it leak oil?"

Suddenly, I turned ashen and hurried outside. How could I have been so stupid? I had driven a thousand miles in a Corvair, a car I had told Benjy was infamous for leaking and burning oil, yet I had been so desperate to get home that I never once checked the oil.

Uttering Hail Marys, I hoisted the engine cover, grabbed the dipstick, and yanked it out. I held it up to the sun and squinted to see if there was even a smidge of oil. Just an iota would relieve my fears. But the stick was bone dry. I fetched the extra quart of oil that Wally had stashed in the front trunk. That quart, plus two more quarts I found in the garage, brought the oil level up to FULL. I was in despair. I had starved the engine of oil. I wondered if I would have to install a new engine before I sold the car.

"You didn't check the oil, did you?" Benjy, still in pajamas, stood outside the front door.

"No, I didn't," I admitted. "I expect this will get me kicked out of the Corvair Brotherhood."

"Why do you even like this car?" he asked, taking a few tentative steps closer.

"At the moment, I don't know if I do like it. Maybe I will start a garden instead. Then at least we'll both eat vegetables."

"No, thank you. No vegetables. You should grow flowers instead."

I sighed and laughed at myself. What a fiasco!

"What?" Benjy asked. "Why are you laughing?"

"Deathmobile," I said. "I now have my very own Deathmobile. Dad would be so happy."

Benjy eyed me gravely, as if I were teetering on the edge of insanity. I explained. "That was the name my friends gave Grandpa's Corvair. The Deathmobile. It was a joke. Because they were so unsafe. Unsafe at any speed."

That threw Benjy for a loop. "That's not a joke. If they were unsafe, then they were Deathmobiles."

"You ever hear of Ralph Nader?" I asked.

"Ralph Nader ran for president on the Green Party ticket in the year 2000 with Winona LaDuke as his running mate, and received almost a hundred thousand votes in Florida," Benjy replied. "Al Gore and Joe Lieberman lost Florida to George W. Bush and Dick Cheney by five hundred thirty-seven votes. Many experts believe that if Nader had not run, Gore would have won Florida, which had twenty-five electoral votes, and he would have become the president instead of Bush."

Clearly, Benjy had heard of Ralph Nader.

"Ralph Nader has run for president multiple times," Benjy continued, reeling off the years, parties, and running mates.

"Back in 1965," I explained once Benjy paused for breath, "before anyone had ever heard of him, Ralph Nader wrote a book called *Unsafe at Any Speed*. He argued that automobile manufacturers could make cars safer. And he was right. In fact, he was so right that the government established an agency to make sure manufacturers made safe cars. So his book helped make cars safer, which was a good thing."

"Yes!" Benjy enthusiastically seconded.

"And in his book Nader cited the Corvair as the most unsafe car built in America. The Corvair had a unique design, very different from other cars. He said that design was flawed, and that it caused deaths and injuries that would not have occurred in those other cars. So, for that reason, my friends called our Corvair the Deathmobile. Lots of people called Corvairs that."

"Then how come Grandpa had one?"

Suddenly, the car interested him, so I gave him the salesman's tour. "Well, let me show you." I waved my hand over the engine. "All other American cars at that time had their engine and transmission in the front and their differential in the rear, so they had a big hump in the center of the floor. But the Corvair had all three in the rear. That design difference saved weight, reduced costs, created more interior room, boosted fuel economy, and improved handling and traction. Dad loved that the car he drove was different and innovative—and cheap to operate. He especially loved that."

"You got your cheapness from him," Benjy said.

"Thank you," I laughed. "Yes, I did. But then Nader said that design difference made the car unsafe, and it became the Deathmobile. Even after the government said it really was safe."

"It really was safe?" Benjy asked.

"The government agency that Nader helped create studied the Corvair, put it through all kinds of tests along with a lot of similar small cars, and found that the Corvair was as safe as or even safer than those similar cars, as long as the tires were properly inflated. Because so much weight was in the rear of a Corvair, its tire pressures had to be different from other cars, and a lot of people didn't realize that."

"So it wasn't really unsafe," Benjy concluded. "It was just different. So people thought there was something wrong with it." He chewed on that thought awhile, as if he liked the taste, then circled the car, nodding. He understood it; he could feel its pain. "It's like me," he said finally.

"What do you mean?" I asked. I knew exactly what he meant, but I wanted to engage him and keep him from thinking about Wheeler.

"There's nothing really wrong with it once you understand it. It's not like it's defective or disabled. It's just different. Like me."

I didn't know if Benjy's analogy was fair or true, and I didn't care. All I knew was we were having a two-way give-and-take dialogue, and I didn't want it to end and have him crawl back into bed. So I asked him to repeat his point to keep him talking.

Word for word, Benjy repeated what he'd just said, then added, "Normals put labels on things that are different, like 'Deathmobile.' Or 'retard.' But just because this car was different, that didn't mean it was worse. It's like I'm different from normals. That doesn't mean I'm worse. I do a lot of things better, like reading and remembering stuff. I'm just different."

"Maybe we should go to McDonald's and continue discussing this over Chicken McNuggets," I suggested. "I want to hear more about it."

He eyed me suspiciously—I'd never before in his 19 years on this earth volunteered to drive him to McDonald's. I couldn't stand the place. But now I'd stoop to anything to keep the conversation going, even McDonald's, so I put the squeeze on. "Since when have you ever passed up Chicken McNuggets? Go upstairs and get dressed and we'll go."

Even though Benjy often had difficulty picking up social cues and the subtext of conversations, this was too blatantly obvious to escape him. He smelled a rat—an ulterior motive. "You actually want to go to McDonald's?"

"I heard they have new stuff on the menu," I said innocently. "Healthy stuff. Salads."

He wasn't buying it. "You don't like vegetables. Besides, it's too early for Chicken McNuggets," he said, starting to head back to the house. "They're only serving breakfast."

"Hey! You're not gonna crawl back under the covers, are you?" I called after him. "We'll get that egg thing." I scoured my memory bank for the catchy name. "An Egg McMuffin!"

"I don't like eggs, Dad," he reminded me.

"Look, by the time you get dressed, and we buy some more oil, and then drive to McDonalds, they'll have the McNuggets," I insisted, as if I knew what I was talking about. "You'll be the first person today to order Chicken McNuggets."

"McDonald's serves Chicken McNuggets in Asia and Europe, Dad, where the clocks are several hours ahead of ours. So I can't be the first person to order them today, because Asians and Europeans have already ordered them today."

"Look," I said impatiently, applying full pressure, "do you want to go or not? This is my final offer. Last call for Chicken McNuggets."

He considered it. "I can get dressed slowly," he finally conceded.

"It's too loud!" Benjy yelled, putting his hands over his ears as I accelerated the Corvair away from our driveway. Like many Aspergians, he was extremely sensitive to loud noises.

"That's because all the weather seals that keep noise out are rotted," I bellowed so he could hear me.

With hands still over ears, he twisted and turned to examine the car. "There are no seat belts in the back!" he shouted.

"They weren't required back when this was built."

"Are you positive this car is safe?" Benjy demanded, still shouting.

I pulled his hand slightly away from his ear. "We've got modern seats, headrests, shoulder harnesses. It's too old to have airbags, unfortunately. But I wouldn't drive us in it if I thought it wasn't safe."

Benjy sighed loudly and slowly uncovered both ears to test whether the sound was bearable. Satisfied, he finally let his hands down. "It's really very loud," he reiterated. "Prolonged exposure to loud noises can damage a person's hearing."

"If we keep it, we'll install new weather seals, and it'll be much quieter."

"Why did you buy it if you're not going to keep it?" Benjy asked.

"Because you're going to be living at home now. For a while at least. If you don't like it, I won't keep it."

He considered it for a moment. "It's okay," he finally said. "It's just too loud."

Wow, I thought, this was interesting. Once Benjy made up his mind about something, trying to get him to change was usually a waste of breath. This was *very* interesting.

When we did errands together, Benjy usually came with me into the stores. But this morning, on our first stop at AutoZone, he decided to wait in the Corvair. As I waddled back out with two cases of 30-weight oil to slake the Corvair's ravenous thirst, I found him giving two country gentlemen a tour of the car. "Almost all other cars at that time had their engine and transmission in the front and their differential in the rear," he told them. "But the Corvair had all three in the rear. That saved weight, created more interior room, boosted fuel economy, and improved handling and traction. It was cheaper to operate. My grandfather and father both like that."

It was almost word for word the salesman's tour I'd given him earlier.

"Your boy sure knows this car," said the gentleman in the John Deere cap.

"Okay if we take a peek at that engine?" asked the gentleman in the CAT cap.

Happy to oblige and also to check the oil again, I raised the rear engine cover. Before I could open my mouth, Benjy resumed his lecture. "There's no radiator," he pointed out, repeating factoids we'd discussed on our drive here. "The engine is made out of aluminum so it doesn't overheat."

"And inside that big, shiny thing," replied CAT, pointing to the stainless steel air cleaner housing atop the engine, "that's where the four hamsters live that spin the wheel to make it go."

"It's a four hamster-power engine, is it?" laughed John Deere.

I grinned. Pretty funny, I thought. But Benjy didn't laugh; he didn't even smile. "There are no hamsters," he said.

"It's a joke," I told him softly. "Engine power is measured in horsepower. So hamster-power is a joke."

"Oh," he said. "Okay."

John Deere and CAT both eyed Benjy with a look that said "I Don't Quite Know What's Different About This Kid, But There is Definitely Something Different." I'd seen it many times, and I responded as I usually did—with a wink. That usually told people all they needed to know and put them at ease.

"Wow! Super-cool car!" squealed the girl at the McDonald's drive-thru window as she handed us Benjy's Chicken McNuggets meal and my cup of water. Fluorescent purple, green, and red locks hung down beneath her cap.

"It's a Corvair!" Benjy shouted across me from the passenger seat, craning his neck to see the girl—and be seen.

"Wow! Neat! What's a Corvair?" She pushed a purple feather-wrapped hair strand back under her cap. "Benjy, is that you? You never told me you had such a cool car!"

"It's actually my Dad's," Benjy said, always a stickler for accuracy. "This is a 1965 Corvair, the first year of the Late Model version, and the same year my grandfather had. Except this is a two-door with a convertible top and his was a four-door without a convertible top. My dad bought it on eBay from a man in Fort Lauderdale, Florida, which is one thousand miles from here. He flew to Atlanta, Georgia, on a regional jet and then changed to another regional jet for the flight to Fort Lauderdale, Florida. Then he drove the car back here, a thousand miles in seventeen hours in a forty-five-year-old car! Some people think this car is defective, but it's just different from a normal car. It's better!"

The girl grinned and nodded on each of Benjy's words while stealing anxious glances at the long line of cars behind us. "That's so awesome!" she said when Benjy finally paused to take a breath. "But I can't talk here, Benjy. I'm kinda supposed to be working."

I put my hand on Benjy's knee to cue him from talking more and said, "We're holding up the line and keeping your friend from doing her job. Maybe you can tell her more at school?"

"Yes! That would be great!" the girl chirped agreeably, pushing her purple locks back under her McDonald's cap again. "Maybe we could go for a ride sometime?"

Benjy poured cold water over that idea. "We can't take you for a ride. There are no seat belts in the back. It's not safe."

"Oh, well!" the girl chirped again. She turned to see if the manager was watching, and he was. She then banged the drive-thru window shut.

"She seemed nice," I purred as I pulled out, trolling for information. "Very friendly."

"I guess," he said, with a mouthful of McNugget. "She never really talked to me before."

"Does she have a name?" I prodded.

"Lydia. We were in the school play together." He swallowed the Mc-Nugget, then asked, "Dad?"

"Yes?"

"I think we need to install seat belts in the back as soon as possible."

"Why is that?" I played dense. "What's the rush?"

"In case we have passengers. We can't have passengers without seat belts in the back."

"So you think we should keep this car?" I asked. "Because it is a really old car."

"It's okay," said Benjy between bites. "It's different. It needs seat belts in the back though."

"All right," I agreed. "We will put seat belts in the back as soon as possible." If this car could keep us talking like this, I was absolutely keeping it.

CHAPTER 7

"It doesn't look like a college the way Wheeler did," Benjy said as we parked at the modest campus of James Monroe Community College.

"Don't stereotype," I told him. "It's not old or ivy-covered, but it's got an excellent reputation, the teachers are supposed to be terrific, it's right down the road so you can live at home, and it'll open the doors to a lot of new and exciting subjects you'll love. And after a year or two here, maybe then you'll transfer to Wheeler or some other school."

We sat down in the Admissions Office and soon heard, "Benjamin, I am so excited to meet you and to hear that you are enrolling at James Monroe!" Full of enthusiasm, Katie Baxter, the Disability Services Coordinator, showed us into her cramped office. "You have a most impressive record, young man!" she chirped, ticking off Benjy's high school grades and accomplishments. "You've already got several James Monroe credits from the dual enrollment courses you're taking in high school and you haven't even started here yet!"

"I wanted to go to Wheeler, but they rejected me," Benjy grumbled. "It's got a special program for Asperger's students who are different, but I'm too different."

Benjy's blunt revelation that James Monroe was not his first choice didn't faze Katie a bit. Her wide, blazing smile never left her, which gave me plenty of time to marvel at her spectacularly white teeth. "We have lots of students who spend a year or two here and then transfer," she explained. "Unlike many large four-year colleges, we don't have graduate students teaching our courses and we don't have hundreds of students listening to lectures in a giant auditorium. We have many excellent teachers leading small classes, which many students prefer, whether they have a disability or not, especially when the cost is a fraction of four-year schools like Wheeler."

"He'll like that," said Benjy, pointing his finger at me. "He's cheap."

Katie roared with laughter. Looking over to me, she caught me staring at her. She slowly dropped her upper lip and eyed me with the look that Benjy usually got, the one that said "I Don't Quite Know What's Different, But There is Definitely Something Different About You."

"Sorry," I apologized, once I realized I was being inappropriate. "Your teeth are great. Really white. I guess I was staring."

"Thank you," Katie replied, awkwardly.

"Not supposed to stare, am I?" I said to Benjy, flushing with embarrassment.

"He has Asperger's too," Benjy explained. "Just not as much as me."

"I see," said Katie, her smile returning, fortunately. In her job, she'd probably seen every behavior imaginable. Soon she was back on track, asking Benjy, "Have you formed any career goals yet?"

"I want to advocate for people who are different," Benjy replied. "Sometimes people who are different are labeled as disabled, and stereotyped and stigmatized, and that's not right."

"You are certainly right about that!" Katie said eagerly. "I'm all about that! You are preaching to the choir. And we have a number of courses—communications, writing, political science, psychology—that will help you pursue that goal. Any other goals we should plan for?"

"I want to live independently," Benjy said. "And I want to be a race car driver. Except the DMV won't allow me to get a driver's license. Which makes it hard for me to live independently and be a race car driver."

After several more paragraphs on the DMV's discrimination against him, he finally paused. "You are already an excellent and passionate advocate!" said Katie, her full smile turned back on. "As for your independent living goal, we're not a residential college, but we do have several Life Skills courses that will certainly help. And as for driving a race car, we do have a few courses in auto repair, but none on driving instruction. You have to go to a private company for that. But has the DMV actually turned you down for a driver's license?"

"No," admitted Benjy. "I haven't tried. There's no point. I know they discriminate."

"Well, you should try," Katie urged. "I have several students with disabilities who have driver's licenses."

"There are principles at stake," insisted Benjy. "People with differences shouldn't have to comply with unfair rules."

Katie nodded solemnly, then smiled at me—perhaps my inappropriateness was forgiven. She moved on to discuss the accommodations and services Benjy could receive at James Monroe. "I have several Asperger's students here, and they do quite well," she assured us. "But you must understand that college is different from high school. As a person with a disability—or a difference—your high school had the obligation to provide you with an appropriate education. But a college doesn't have that same obligation. Here you will need to take the initiative to ask for help and accommodations. And when I say you, I mean you, not your father. You are the student and you are responsible for your education."

Benjy nodded. "He doesn't help me much anyway," he said.

"Good!" Katie exploded, winking at me. "Taking on that responsibility will help you to live independently. You're already making progress toward your goals!" She flipped through Benjy's high school transcript. Then her smile dimmed. "I see that you will need to take our math assessment."

I cringed, recalling hours upon agonizing hours of frustrating homework and baffling tests. Some people with Asperger's or autism are whizzes at math; a few, like Kim Peek, the real-life inspiration for Dustin Hoffman's character in the movie *Rain Man*, are even savants. But that was not Benjy. Math for him usually consisted of scrawling illegible numbers indecipherably up, down, and around a piece of paper, followed by erasing so furious that the paper often ripped, so that he had to start over again. "Benjy has a diagnosed learning disability in math," I explained. "It has always been hugely challenging for him. Despite that, he worked incredibly hard and passed the state's standardized tests in Algebra I and II. Doesn't he get credit for that?"

Katie spoke directly to Benjy. "All students here have to pass one college-level math course to receive a diploma. That's a requirement for students at most colleges. Including Wheeler. What you'll take now is simply an assessment. It tells us if an incoming student is prepared for the required college-level math course or needs some remedial work first. You've already passed those algebra courses, so I'm sure you'll do fine." She smiled encouragingly.

Benjy's chin dropped to his chest as if his neck had suddenly snapped.

After we left Katie's office, his gloom was as deep as when he had been rejected by Wheeler. "I hate math," he said finally, once we were safely inside the Corvair.

"It'll be okay," I said. "It's just one course. I can help if you want."

"You don't know any math," Benjy said. "Mom always had to help me."

It was true. We both knew Benjy's math disability had come straight from me.

"College is supposed to be courses I want to take. So I can do what I want to do," he said as we pulled out of the parking lot.

"They have some required courses. It's no big deal." But it was a huge deal to him; he had pictured college as an invigorating journey from one mesmerizing topic to the next, each unlocking engaging new worlds to him. Instead, he faced a forced march through a subject he had barely survived in high school.

"Did you take math in college?" he asked.

"Yes."

"And you don't know any now. So what's the point?"

"The point is I learned enough to pass the course," I said. "So can you. And then you can forget it if you want, just like I did, because you probably won't ever need to use it."

"That's not the point, Dad!"

"The point is math is required," I said. "They want you to have a complete education—to be a well-rounded, educated young man.

Really, it's not a big deal. I know you can do it. You've already done it."

"So why do I have to do it again?" he exclaimed.

"I don't know."

Benjy stared out the window for the rest of the ride home. As we arrived, he asked, "Can we get the seatbelts for the back now?"

"Benjy, come on," I said as I turned off the Corvair. "So you'll take this test and then you'll take one math course. It's not the end of the world, it's the beginning. Look at the bright side. You are going to college. You'll have fine teachers and wonderful opportunities."

He hopped out the passenger door and stormed inside.

The next day, I nosed the Corvair carefully along a gravel road, avoiding large potholes, small sinkholes, and chickens skittering everywhere. The houses ran the gamut from single-wide to double-wide; some were level and neat while others had fallen, exhausted, off their cinder block foundations. In the front yards, goats roamed among rusted tractors and old cars. A gray hound lazing peacefully on the asphalt lifted his head, then dropped it back down as we slowly maneuvered around him; judging by the ad we were answering on Craigslist that offered to sell nearly a hundred Corvairs, either whole or in parts, this hound had probably seen so many Deathmobiles creep by over the years that ours wasn't worth a second glance.

At the END STATE MAINTENANCE sign, the gravel gave way to a red clay path pockmarked by moon-sized craters. Scrawled in red, a sign ordered KEEP OUT! THIS MEANS YOU! We were less than an hour from home, but it was a different world.

"You sure about these directions?" I asked. I checked my cell phone to see if I had reception in case we were lost. There was no service; we had strayed too far off the beaten path into a hardscrabble landscape that hadn't changed in decades.

"Road becomes driveway," Benjy read from my notes.

We ignored the warning sign and pushed deeper into the wilderness. As the path disintegrated into two barely discernible mud tracks, the Corvair's front end spoiler bashed down again and again, even though I was barely crawling.

"You shouldn't have been so cheap, Dad," Benjy said. "You should've just bought the parts online from Clark's Corvair Parts. They have eight buildings of Corvair parts." He had me pegged. That's why I was here; I thought I could score a deal. But destroying my Corvair to save a few bucks on parts for it was starting to seem like a not so great idea. As I searched for a place to turn around, a frame farmhouse came into view. At one time, the siding appeared to have been white, but paint had been estranged from it for decades, replaced by mildew. The square red barn was in better shape; it looked sturdy enough to remain standing for at least another week. A Corvair rested near the barn door. It had been light blue when it was built but was now a new color: rust. "That's an Early Model Corvair," Benjy said.

"We must be in the right place," I said unenthusiastically, while aiming our Late Model at a dry island among the puddles where we could park. Neither of us was eager to get out. "We'll just get the parts we need and be on our way," I told Benjy. "You can wait in the car if you want."

"I'm okay," he claimed.

Out of the car, we picked our steps carefully to avoid mud that would swallow our shoes. Just then, three gray and hungry hounds exploded from the barn, barking like banshees and homing in on Benjy, poised to attack. He covered his ears, turned purple, and burst into hysterical wails. He had always been terrified by any animal that jumped or barked at him; we were one of the few families in America in which a child begged us to *not* get a puppy. I jumped over a puddle to get between him and kicked out to make the dogs back off; they gave ground but kept baying and baring their teeth as if we were foxes.

"GET THEM AWAY!" Benjy screamed. We both feared one wrong move would make the hounds lunge and bite.

"MANNY! Get yer sorry tail over here!" a husky voice growled from the barn doorway. As if a switch had been thrown, the lead dog stopped barking and trotted back to the voice. The other two meekly followed.

"Hell, it's only dogs," said the voice, now growling at us.

I saw a man in a wheelchair at the door of the barn. The dogs dropped to the ground beside him and awaited his next command.

Benjy was hyperventilating now, struggling to catch his breath and calm down. I edged him back toward our Corvair. "We'll come back another time," I lied to the man. I had no intention of ever coming back.

"Suit yourself," he said. "These dogs won't trouble you no more. Unless you trouble them. Or me."

Benjy resisted my pushing him. "I'm okay," he said. I turned and looked him in the eye. The purple in his face had softened to beet red.

"We can order seat belts from Clark's," I told him.

He looked to the man in his chair, and his resolve stiffened. "I'm okay," he repeated.

We cautiously resumed our tiptoeing between puddles to reach the barn, and the dogs didn't stir. I introduced ourselves and explained, "Benjy's not a dog person."

"Kenny Dettor," he spit out at us, not offering his hand to shake. "These dogs wouldn't hurt a fly unless I told them to. They's well-trained." He seemed put out by the commotion. From underneath his "What's Saddam Funny?" cap, his long, jet-black hair fell over his shoulders. He couldn't have been more than a few years older than Benjy, yet his gaunt, bearded face was wrinkled and worn. Abruptly spinning his chair around, he wheeled himself to a John Deere Gator, adroitly swung his body from the chair to the seat and spun the vehicle around, showering our pants with mud. "Hop on," he ordered.

I sat beside Kenny in the center of the bench seat and Benjy squeezed in beside me. Kenny punched the Gator's gas, rooster-tailing muddy water while seemingly aiming for the deepest potholes on the way to the field behind the barn. I threw my arm around Benjy's shoulder and braced myself to keep from flying out. Then I begged Kenny to slow down.

"We're here," he replied gruffly. But all I could see were overgrown weeds and brush.

"It's Corvairs," said Benjy. Camouflaged within the overgrowth, nose to bumper and door to door, their tires flattened by time, were the hundred dead Corvairs that Kenny had advertised for sale.

"You've got quite an unusual crop," I joked lamely. Kenny didn't crack a smile. "How did you get all these?" I asked.

"I didn't," Kenny grunted. "My father did. People gave 'em to him if he'd haul 'em away. Then we'd fix 'em up and sell 'em, whole or parts. Had a pretty good business. But he's gone now over a year. And since I'm now gonna be in this chair awhile, like the rest of my life, I ain't real interested in carryin' it on."

"I'm sorry," I said. "May I ask what happened?"

"Iraq happened," he said, then spit into the mud. "An I.E.D. happened." Kenny saw Benjy's blank look and explained. "Improvised Explosive Device. It blew up under our Humvee, which then rolled over on me, and that was all she wrote for my spine." He spit into the mud again. "Take whatever you want before they go to the crusher. I'll be in the barn. We'll settle up there."

"There were supposed to be weapons of mass destruction in Iraq," Benjy said, "but it turned out there weren't any."

"Hell, yes, there were," Kenny fired back. "They was called I.E.D.s and Humvees."

"Thank you for your service and sacrifice," I said as we slid out of the Gator.

"You're so very welcome," he muttered bitterly, then punched the Gator's pedal, again rooster-tailing mud as he drove off.

I explained to Benjy that many American soldiers serving in Iraq had been injured when I.E.D.s exploded under their Humvees and other military vehicles. He nodded, and we walked on in silence among the rusting Corvairs. To break the silence, I told him what I knew of them. There were Early Models from the 1960 to 1964 model years, Late Models from 1965 to 1969, two-doors, four-doors, convertibles, and turbocharged coupes. There were rare Corvair models such as the Lakewood station wagon, with the air-cooled engine under the rear cargo floor, and the Greenbrier window van, America's first minivan. There was even a telephone company's old Corvair pickup truck, the Rampside; a passenger side's drop-down ramp allowed cargo to be rolled up from the ground into the bed.

"This is a treasure trove of Corvair history," I told Benjy. "I saw a YouTube video where an elephant walked up a Rampside's ramp. It was amazing." Unfortunately, all the vehicles were crammed full of motors, wheels, axles, differentials, and other Corvair detritus—everything except seat belts. The weather seals I found were rotted worse than the ones already on our car.

I noticed Benjy kept looking back at the barn. "Do you think Kenny lives independently?" he finally asked.

"I don't know," I replied. "But he's so unfriendly, it's hard to picture anyone living with him."

We returned to the barn, empty-handed, and found Kenny drinking a beer beside a hot red Late Model two-door coupe, up on jack stands with all its trim and wheels on the dirt floor.

"A hundred Corvairs and you didn't find nothin'?" Kenny growled, then spit. "You come down here and kick tires, wastin' my time? It ain't easy for me to get around, in case you ain't noticed." As his voice became angrier, Manny, Moe, and Jack perked their heads up from the floor and glared at us.

"I was looking for rear seat belts and the cars were so full of stuff, I didn't see any," I explained. As Benjy eyed the dogs warily, I put my hand around his shoulder.

"Look in the boxes against the back wall. Over there." Kenny slung his can in the direction he wanted us to go and beer splashed into his lap. He cursed, guzzled what remained, crumpled up the can, and tossed it into a tall pile of other empties.

I didn't want Benjy to be left with this picture of a bitter and angry man with a disability, so I tried to draw Kenny out. "You look like you're restoring that one," I said pointing to the red Corvair. "It's gorgeous."

"My father started it. Every now and then I put a wrench to it. You want it? Make me an offer, it's all for sale. And no lowballs. I'll put the dogs to anyone tries to lowball me."

"I don't think you should crush those cars out there," blurted out Benjy. "Corvairs were different from other cars. They—"

"Save it!" Kenny loudly interrupted. "I've heard it, okay? From my dad and all his lame Corvair buddies. You pay me two hundred each, haul 'em away, and you can open your museum. I don't want 'em. I need the money."

Shocked by Kenny's hostility, Benjy, for the first time I could remember, did not finish making his point. I quickly led him away to search the boxes at the back. Hopefully, we'd find a few things to buy to make Kenny happy, then flee as fast as the Corvair could take us. Burrowing into the first box among the bulbs, belts, gaskets, and other parts, I soon struck pay dirt: weather seals for the doors, new in the package. I dug further and found new seat belts, plus the hardware to anchor them. In another box, I found oil and air filters. Then I struck the mother lode: a new set of hard-to-find weather seals for my convertible top. Now, when I drove the Corvair with the top up, I wouldn't need ear plugs. We hadn't wasted Kenny's time after all, or ours.

"Dad?" I heard Benjy call, tremblingly, from around a corner. Assuming the dogs were menacing him, I dropped everything and ran over, but they weren't there. Instead, I found him staring at a Late Model Corvair with the legs of two men and a woman sticking out from its closed front end trunk. The car had been painted as a man-eating shark, with its jaws clamped down on the waists of its victims, its huge teeth biting them in two, as if swallowing their heads and torsos while leaving their legs dangling.

Benjy gasped for breath and I held him, assuring him, "It's a joke! A prank! It's not real!"

Now, Manny, Moe, and Jack came over, growling and with bared teeth, to investigate his hyperventilating. "GET THEM AWAY!" Benjy screamed. It was all too much; he was suffering a full-blown meltdown.

The three howling hounds stopped at Benjy's feet, snarling, until Kenny commanded "SHUSH!" He slowly rolled his chair over, as if he could scarcely be bothered. The dogs lay down at Benjy's feet and glared at him, waiting for him to make one wrong move.

Benjy whimpered. Terror had turned his face bright purple again.

"Get a grip, will ya?" demanded Kenny. He wheeled to the shark Corvair's trunk, lifted the lid, and the bottom halves of the three mannequins dropped to the dirt floor. "It's a gag my Dad and I did. To make it look like the Vair ate the people. They're dummies!"

Benjy nodded over and over, but couldn't stop gasping.

"It's just a joke," I said, trying to soothe him. "The Corvair's a Killer Car. It's like a man-eating shark, it eats people. Get it? It's funny."

Benjy gobbled air deep into his lungs, trying to calm himself. But it didn't come quickly enough for Kenny. He rolled his eyes in exasperation. "Hey, Kid, I mean, first it's the dogs, then it's the dummies. Maybe you should join the Army? I did when I was your age. You get to serve yer country. And you might lose your legs, but you'll sure grow some balls."

Now I was the one who turned purple. "Hey!" I exploded. "Don't you ever speak to my son that way! You don't know him!"

"I know him to be one weird pussy," Kenny sneered.

"If you weren't in that chair," I seethed, my finger in Kenny's face, "and hadn't served this country, I would punch your lights out. You think you're superior? At least he doesn't let his disability make him bitter and angry. You should learn from him, not mock him."

"You gonna buy those parts or not?" Kenny demanded unapologetically.

"You sonova—!" As the dogs stood and growled at me, I bit my tongue and counted to five. "I sincerely hope you get the help you need," I finally said in the most dog-soothing voice I could manage, "because you really, really need help." I dropped the parts in Kenny's lap and, praying he wouldn't command his dogs to follow us, hustled Benjy out to the car.

CHAPTER 8

"You shouldn't have yelled at Kenny," Benjy said as we pitched back and forth while I sped the Corvair down the driveway and into one mud crater after another, fleeing Kenny's house as fast as I could without breaking the car's suspension. "Maybe he can't help being like that."

"I'm sure he can help it, and I don't want to talk about him ever again," I sputtered. "The only good thing I can say about him is that he didn't order his dogs to attack us."

"OWWW," cried Benjy, after a huge pothole caused our heads to bounce against the metal superstructure of the Corvair's rag top. "Slow down! I hit my head! It might be broken!"

Seeing there wasn't anyone following us, I throttled back. "Sorry," I said.

Finally, the car reached the gravel road and I accelerated again. We had made our getaway and I could relax. Instead, I choked up. "I'm just so sorry for bringing you down here. I admire your forgiving him, Benjy, but I can't. No one has the right to speak to you or anyone else that way, disability or not."

"You should say difference, Dad, not disability." Benjy stared out the window as usual, as if nothing had just happened.

"I know you know this already," I said, "but there are people in this world who will tease you because they don't understand you and make no effort to understand you. Like the bullies on the long bus. And that's Kenny—he's a bully. It's not your fault, it's his. Not everyone can be good." I looked over at Benjy; he still stared out the window.

When we finally reached the main highway, I punched the gas pedal, and the Corvair lurched forward.

"You're speeding, Dad," Benjy warned as he was pushed back into his seat. "Slow down."

"You're right," I admitted. I let up on the gas. I hadn't floored the Corvair before. Pretty impressive acceleration, I thought.

"I'm glad we came here," Benjy said. "It wasn't so bad. We saw a lot of Corvairs."

After the debacle with Kenny, I ordered the seat belts and other parts from Clark's Corvair Parts ("world's largest Corvair parts supplier, over 15,000 Corvair parts in stock!"). The service was friendly, the package arrived quickly, the instructions seemed straightforward, and, best of all, there was no Kenny. Never again would I try to save a buck on Corvair parts.

The following Saturday, after Benjy finished his NASCAR game, I recruited him to help install the seat belts. "I could use an assistant. Interested?"

I had no illusions that he'd join me. Nearly every weekend for the past decade, I had invited Benjy to assist me with household and yard chores. More than the help he might provide, however, I'd hoped it would be time when we could yak and joke and talk father-son talk; if he actually helped me, it would be a bonus. I had learned over all the years I'd tried to recruit him, however, that he did not like chores that involved dirty, yucky, sharp, or smelly stuff, getting into uncomfortable positions, or using metal objects like screwdrivers that raised any possibility of an injury or bleeding—in other words, nearly all household chores. He always politely declined my invitation, saying, "No, thank you."

"Sure," he said this time.

Wow! Okay! I rushed us both into work clothes before he changed his mind, then gave him the installation instructions to review.

Benjy read the directions and had second thoughts. "Maybe we ought to have a professional do this, Dad?" he asked in his usual flat tone.

"I thought we were going to do it together. What happened?"

"It looks too hard for you."

"It looks easy to me," I said, only mildly offended. "Clark's said it was easy."

"You have to drill. Drills are sharp and can cut people so they bleed."

"Don't worry about the drilling," I assured him. "I can handle the drilling."

He was un-persuaded. "Seat belts are for safety. If we don't do it right, they might not be safe."

"We have instructions," I protested. "A diagram. I feel confident. People on the Corvair Forum on the Internet say this is not hard. If you read the instructions to me as I work, I think we'll be fine."

"You're not mechanical, Dad. You say that all the time. If you bleed on the car, it could rust. Corvairs are prone to rust." He was digging in.

"I know. But part of the fun of owning an old car is working on it and improving it. It's the satisfaction of solving problems with your mind and your own two hands as you bring a classic vehicle back to life. It's becoming one with the machine."

He looked at me quizzically. "If it's a machine, Dad, you can't become one with it, because you are not a machine."

"It's just a metaphor," I said. "It's sort of a Zen thing—by fixing and rehabilitating a car, you become spiritually one with it."

"It's a car, Dad," Benjy insisted. "It's an inanimate object. It doesn't have a spirit."

"Look," I said firmly, "I'm doing this. I want to learn to become more mechanical. And this is an easy job. It's a good way to begin. Okay? So I'm starting. I'm using my new hydraulic jack to lift the car up onto my new jack stands so I can work underneath it."

"You're going under the car?" Benjy wasn't often incredulous; this was an exception. "What if it falls on you?"

"It won't fall on me," I said, jacking quickly.

"Are you sure you're not just being cheap?"

"I'm sure," I replied testily, jacking faster, venting my frustration with his lack of confidence in my mechanical talents. "I did work at a service station once, you know. When I was your age."

"You only pumped gas, Dad."

"I also did some light mechanical work, okay? Can we just get started, please?" I locked the last two jack stands under the car and released the jack. The car dropped with a thud onto the stands. "See?" I said proudly. "We're jacked up and ready to go. First instruction, please."

Benjy relented and read the first instruction: "Remove the rear seat."

"Okay," I said, pleased. "Now we're off and running. This will be a first. I've never removed the rear seat of a car before." With the Corvair now secure atop four jack stands, I climbed into the elevated rear of the car, bent down, took a deep breath, grunted, and mightily yanked up on the rear seat cushion. It turned out to be light as a feather and unsecured, causing me to lose my balance and crash against the back of the driver's seat, which in turn crashed against the steering wheel, which caused the horn to honk, long and loud.

"DAD!" Benjy yelled, covering his ears.

I stood up and the horn stopped honking. "Everything's fine," I said unsteadily.

"Maybe we ought to have a professional do this, Dad," Benjy again suggested, a bit more insistently.

Even though I'd wrenched my back painfully, I again refused, and, with the seat cushion out, examined 45 years of accumulated dirt and gunk. "Maybe we should call a professional—a professional archaeologist, ha ha," I joked.

"I meant a different kind of professional, Dad," Benjy said. "A professional automobile mechanic," he added, in case I hadn't understood.

We'd come to the tricky part: drilling the holes through the rear metal panel of the passenger compartment into where the engine, transmission, differential, and lots of other important things lived. As Benjy started to suggest going to a professional again, he accurately read my social cue—a penetrating glare that unmistakably said, "Do not even think about asking me that question again!"—and stopped himself. Instead, he reread the instructions to me, and I successfully located four slight nail punches in the panel—tiny marks that a worker on GM's Body by Fisher assembly line had punched decades earlier to guide someone like me in the event he someday decided to install the then-optional rear seat belts. Ever so cautiously, I drilled the first hole for the seat belt anchor bolts, silently praying that the Body by Fisher man would not lead me astray and I would not cut anything useful like, say, a brake or fuel line. After what seemed an eternity, the drill broke through and the bit suddenly lunged toward the engine. I stopped the drill and slowly reversed the bit back, hoping to avoid an explosion. It didn't come. We had survived long enough to drill a second hole. But I needed a minute; my hand clutching the drill was trembling.

For the next three bolts, Benjy repeated the instructions word for word as I carefully drilled. He wasn't reading, of course. He had memorized them the first time. With all four bolt holes finished, I had successfully avoided blowing us up.

"Still think we need professional help?" I teased. I raised my hand for a high five.

"Maybe we ought to have a professional do this, Dad," Benjy repeated, as flat as before, while ignoring my high-five invite. My skills had not impressed him.

"Do you want to go underneath or stay up here in the rear of the car?" I asked.

"If I go under the car," he said, "it could fall on me." I armed him with a pair of locking pliers and had him take my place in the back of the car. I then slid under the car on my new creeper. With my snout just a few claustrophobic inches beneath the underbody of the car, Benjy's "It could fall on me" reverberated in my ears. I worked nervously yet purposefully, as if defusing a ticking time bomb. As I pushed each bolt through a wide washer and then through the hole in the rear panel, I called for Benjy to grab it, put a belt anchor, washer, and nut on it, then lock the pliers on the nut while I tightened the bolt from below.

"OWWW!" he suddenly hollered.

"WHAT?!" I hollered back from below.

"MY KNEES! I CAN'T FIT BACK HERE! I'M TALLER THAN YOU!"

"Shift around," I suggested. "Or hold the pliers from the front seat."

"I HAVE SIZE THIRTEEN FEET, DAD! I'M STUCK!" Then he suddenly changed his tune, shouting, "I'M OKAY! I'M FINE!"

And then, as we moved from bolt to bolt, he yelled "OWWWW" again, and repeated the same cycle of complaints, in the same order.

For the few minutes it took to tighten the four bolts, we bellowed constantly at each other. Then I crept out from under the car, stood up, and extricated him from the back seat.

"I think we did it, dude!"

"I guess," he answered, nonplussed.

I demanded a more exuberant celebration. "With our own hands and minds we actually installed these seat belts, and didn't have to rely on some professional to do it for us!" I exulted. "I thought it would.take all day, and it was less than an hour! Isn't that tremendously satisfying? Don't you feel a great sense of accomplishment? Or maybe a calm, Zen-like inner satisfaction?"

"I guess," he said. Then he added, "You probably saved a lot of money."

"It's not about the money!" I insisted. "It's about personal fulfill-ment—pride in doing your own work and solving your own problems. I'm wired. I want to do more. Let's rotate the tires!"

"Maybe we ought to have a professional do that, Dad."

"Compared to what we just accomplished, it's a walk in the park. We've already got the car jacked up. C'mon, whaddya say?"

"No, thank you," he said politely, "I'm bushed." He returned to the house.

An uneventful tire rotation later, I was lowering the Corvair off the jack stands when Benjy returned. "Y'know how you said we should feel pumped up and proud?" he said. "I think we should celebrate. McDon-ald's will begin serving Chicken McNuggets in nineteen minutes." He fixed his brown eyes on me, his face an open book; he had more than Chicken McNuggets on his mind.

"You have to go—I can't talk to you," Lydia whispered with quiet urgency as she made change for us at her drive-thru window. She sneaked a glance back at her manager. "He nearly fired me the last time you were here, and he'll recognize this car."

"We have the seat belts installed in the back," Benjy whispered back, leaning across me.

"Yo, Benjy, you don't whisper," Lydia whispered. "Only me. So the manager doesn't hear me. If you whisper, I can't hear you."

"Do you want to go for a ride?" Benjy boomed. "We have seat belts in back now so it's safe."

Hearing Benjy's bellow, the manager looked up at Lydia. "I get off in two hours," she hissed, then slammed the window shut.

When Benjy was much younger, Annie had arranged play dates for him, and it wasn't easy. To Benjy, a play date didn't mean playing games or activities that involved interaction with other children. It meant reciting his stories to a captive and sometimes unappreciative audience. Second dates were rare. Then Benjy reached the age where boys didn't do play dates anymore. There were no birthday party invitations, no calls, no e-mails. It wasn't that Benjy had no interest in friends; after rehearsals for the school play, I would see him hovering eagerly around his fellow actors, hoping to join in their conversations. But, despite years of professional and parental social coaching, the fine art of making friends still eluded him.

So there was no way I was now going to blow this opportunity for him to make a friend. We found a shady spot in the McDonald's parking lot, put the convertible top down, ate our lunch, and prepared to wait two hours for Lydia.

Within minutes, however, a steady stream of humanity visited us with questions to ask, stories to tell, or insults to deliver about the Corvair. After wolfing down his McNuggets and fries, Benjy hopped out of the car to give tours. The conversations went like this:

Several Baby Boomers: "My dad (or mom or granddad) had a Corvair. They were cool." Benjy: "Many people owned Corvairs. Nearly one-point-eight million Corvairs were built by GM over ten model years starting with the 1960 model. My grandfather had a blue 1965 Monza four-door with the Powerglide transmission," etc.

Another Boomer: "Unsafe at any speed. Right? The car Nader hated?" Benjy: "This car is different, not defective. In 1972, after testing the Corvair against comparable cars, the United States Government issued a report that said the Corvair was as safe or safer than...," etc.

Three Harley riders in leathers: "Nader! That [expletive deleted]! It's cuz of guys like him that we gotta wear [expletive deleted] helmets." Benjy: "That is not nice language. My mother said people use bad language because they have an 'abject failure of imagination.' She told me to look up 'abject' in the dictionary, because I didn't know what it meant. It means 'extremely bad' or 'miserable' or 'degrading.'" At this point, I quickly intervened.

Teens on skateboards: "Cool car. What is it?" Benjy: "A Corvair. It's the most innovative car made in America in the past fifty years," etc.

Classic Mustang driver: "A hundred bucks says I can kick your car's tail at any distance and on any course you choose." Benjy: "I don't gamble. But your car is not as innovative as the Corvair. The Corvair is the most innovative ...," etc.

A Porsche owner: "I hear Jay Leno calls it the American Porsche. Anyone who thinks that must have never driven a Porsche." Benjy: "Who is Jay Leno? What's a Porsche?"

In what seemed like a blink, the two hours had passed, and Lydia slunk covertly out of McDonald's, still in her uniform. "I don't want the manager to see me," she explained. "He'd probably fire me." And then, "Thanks for the ride, by the way. I needed it. This is awesome."

As I held the seat back for her to climb in the rear, she took off her hat like it was a pair of handcuffs and shook out her hair. It was jet black, other than those hot fluorescent locks up front. I hopped behind the wheel and pulled smartly out of the parking lot.

"Top down! Super awesome!" Lydia buckled the new seat belt and told us where she lived. "I've never ridden in a convertible before," she confessed.

"You're the first person to use that seat belt," Benjy said.

"Well, I am honored," she chirped, then exulted, "Yee Haw! Blue sky and Blue Ridge!" She breathed deeply, then twisted and turned to see everything. "We should write a song with that title." She took her hair clips out and let her hair blow in the breeze.

"I don't know how to write a song," said Benjy.

"Neither do I," admitted Lydia. "We're not gonna let that stop us, are we?"

"No!" agreed Benjy. He paused to consider what to say next. "Because the Corvair has the engine, transmission, and differential in the back, there's no hump in the floor," he finally offered. "They call the transmission and differential together the transaxle." I realized he'd spent more time researching the Corvair than I had, and was glad to show off what he'd learned.

"It is very roomy back here," Lydia agreed. "Much more comfortable than my mother's Prius. Of course, I have to sit behind her big, fat, stupid new husband. She has to drive him, cuz his license got suspended for DUI."

"My mother died," said Benjy matter-of-factly. "Because she didn't get a flu shot, she got the flu, and after she went to the hospital, she got a big infection called sepsis and her organs failed."

I cringed. We had been driving just four minutes. That was waaaaay too much information too soon, I thought. It risked being a conversation stopper for all eternity.

"That's so sad," Lydia said, reaching over the seat to touch Benjy's shoulder. "I am so sorry."

"Senior citizens and kids were supposed to get flu shots then," Benjy explained. "She took me to get one but she didn't get one."

"So she sacrificed hers so a child or senior could have one," said Lydia. "She was, like, a hero."

Suddenly, with tears in my eyes and a big lump in my throat, I liked Lydia a lot. I sneaked a peek over at Benjy, and he stared out to the side as he usually did, betraying no emotion. "She was a heroine, not a hero," he corrected.

"Right! Heroine!" nodded Lydia, grinning. "You're a nice person, Benjy," she said after a moment. "I could see that when we did the play. How come you didn't come to any of the cast parties?"

"I didn't know about them," Benjy said.

"Well, that sucks. Aren't you on Facebook? Wasn't your e-mail address on the cast list?"

"I'm not on Facebook, and I don't have an e-mail."

"I wish I'd known, I would have told you. But I didn't know you didn't know. Next play, you're there."

"Okay!" Benjy said. "Except I'm a senior," he realized. "I'm graduating. There won't be a next time."

"Then that super sucks."

"In the fall, I'm going to James Monroe Community College."

"I might go there, too! I hear it's really good, and it's all I can afford."

"It's not Dartmouth or Wheeler," Benjy said. "And they make you take math. But it is much cheaper."

"Math?" Lydia groaned. "Haven't they heard of calculators and computers?"

My sentiments exactly! Gawd, I hoped she'd be a friend to Benjy. I checked my gas gauge, wanting to drive them both forever.

"Does this car have a name?" Lydia asked.

"It's called a Corvair," answered Benjy. "A Corvair Monza, to be precise."

"But you know how some people give their cars people names? Like Herbie was the name of the Love Bug? Like they're a member of their family?"

"I don't believe in anthropomorphizing inanimate objects like cars," declared Benjy.

"Oh," said Lydia, grinning, without a clue about what Benjy had just said. "Me either."

"Corvair is a good name," Benjy reaffirmed.

"Corvair is an outstanding name," Lydia confirmed.

Their conversation flagged and Lydia gazed out to the mountains, still nodding, still grinning, as if exploring a peaceful new refuge.

Benjy finally broke their silence. "Before the Corvair, in 1948, the Tucker Torpedo also had the engine and transmission in the rear," he said, "but the big car companies put Tucker out of business because Tuckers were more innovative. There was a movie made about it in 1988. It starred Jeff Bridges and was directed by Francis Ford Coppola. Since there were only 51 Tuckers built, I think the Corvair should be considered the most innovative car."

As Benjy regaled Lydia with increasingly obscure details about the wonders of the Corvair, my attention turned to a new sound from the back rear—a metallic pinging and rolling, as if a marble was loose somewhere. What the heck was that? Did we leave some nuts and bolts loose under the rear seat when we were installing the seat belts?

"In 1965, Ralph Nader said the Corvair was unsafe at any speed," Benjy was saying. "He said it killed people. But he wasn't talking about the Late Model, he was talking about the Early Model. This is a Late Model. And what he said wasn't even true about the Early Model. It wasn't true about any Corvairs. It just got stereotyped because it was different. People shouldn't do that."

"I don't like riding in our Prius," Lydia said. "They recalled it and say they fixed it so it won't accelerate out of control now. But what if it did just go crazy on its own? How scary would that be?"

"Our other car is a Toyota Camry," said Benjy. "It got recalled too. I don't like it. It's not different. I only like different cars."

Behind me, the pinging and rolling grew louder. We were on a busy four-lane highway without a place to pull off. Fortunately, less than a mile ahead was an exit with a service station where I could check it out.

"My dad's friends called his father's Corvair a Deathmobile," Benjy said. "They didn't know it wasn't true."

Lydia laughed. "That's funny! Deathmobile!"

A loud CLANK suddenly shot out from underneath Lydia. The driver's side rear wheel wobbled, and we lurched from side to side.

"What's going on?" Lydia asked anxiously. "What's happening?"

"We'll stop at the end of the exit ramp to check it out," I assured her as I swerved into the exit lane. I couldn't stop sooner; there was no shoulder, and traffic was racing up behind me.

The lurching grew worse, pitching us from side to side. "What's happening?!" repeated Lydia, unnerved. In the rear view mirror, I saw the color drain out of her face.

The car weaved back and forth like a drunk on a bender. "Dad, I think something's wrong," said Benjy, his voice flat as usual.

"We'll be fine," I said, exiting the highway while doing my best impression of cool-as-a-cucumber pilot Sully Sullenberger safely landing his airplane in the Hudson River. "But brace yourselves, just in case." Benjy wedged his arms against the glove box and ducked down. Behind my seat, Lydia assumed the crash position.

I slowly wrangled the Corvair into the gas station, parked, yanked up the brake, and shut off the engine. "Safe and sound," I assured all. "Sorry for the unexpected excitement."

Benjy got out of his crash position and seemed okay. Lydia, however, was quietly murmuring, "Oh God, Oh God, Oh God," over and over, rocking back and forth to calm herself.

"I'm sorry," I told her. "I'm really sorry. But we're fine now. Really." Lydia nodded, but kept repeating her *Oh God* mantra.

After I extricated myself from the Corvair, I saw the tilted rear wheel. Removing the wire wheel cover, I discovered that two of the five lug nuts were sheared off completely. A few more revolutions and the wheel might have snapped off the car. Clearly, I had somehow managed to botch the simple task of rotating the tires by not properly tightening the lug nuts. This morning's supremely satisfying Zen moment had become this afternoon's near-death experience.

I offered my hand to Lydia to help her out of the car. "Want to stretch your legs, get something to drink? We'll have some time before the tow truck comes."

Lydia leaped out of the car as if it was on fire. "It *is* a Deathmobile!" she cried.

I looked over to Benjy. Corvair kaput…Lydia mad…. His chin fell to his chest. This wasn't what he'd hoped for.

CHAPTER 9

The wrecker driver carefully dropped the Corvair's rear wheel drum onto a cinder block in front of our garage, capping off a mortifying return to the scene of this morning's triumphant seat belt installation. Before leaving, he handed me his business card. "You'll need it," he advised. In a few hours, I'd fallen from the euphoria of nominating myself to the Mechanics' Hall of Fame down to the humiliation of needing my own personal on-call-around-the-clock tow truck.

Inside, I found Benjy in his bedroom, buried under the covers. As soon as the wrecker stopped in our driveway, he had raced dejectedly straight into the house. "How ya doin'?" I asked.

"Fine." He sounded Not Fine.

"I apologize again for the wheel almost falling off. I'm really, really sorry."

From under the covers, I heard nothing.

"Lydia is really nice, I think." Still nothing. "Wanna talk?"

"No, thank you."

I left him alone and headed to my office to catch up on work.

Two hours later, I heard him race downstairs and go outside, which he rarely did. Peering out the window, I saw a wheelchair beside my Corvair, which was now resting on jack stands. A man's legs stuck out from under the car, looking like the mannequin legs in Kenny's barn.

"What's going on?" I asked Benjy when I got outside.

"I called a professional automobile mechanic and asked him to fix the Corvair," Benjy said.

"You called Kenny? Why did you call Kenny?"

"Because we should have a professional automobile mechanic do this. You are not a professional."

"I see. So you asked him to fix the broken wheel? Gave him our address?"

"Yes." He eyed me with his big browns. "When I called, he said he was really sorry about being mean to me, and for the stuff he said, and that he was glad I called him. He said he sometimes gets in really bad moods. Because of his legs and post-traumatic stress disorder."

"I see. You don't usually use the phone, Benjy."

"The woman at James Monroe said I had to take the initiative. His phone number was in the Craigslist ad on the Internet."

I sighed. "Hello," I finally said to the legs sticking out from beneath the car. "Kenny, could you come out here a second?"

"Looks like someone did a nice job rebuilding this engine," Kenny replied from under the car. "Not leaking a drop of oil."

I still had thoughts of punching him. "Look, please come out here. I appreciate you coming, but I don't want you to fix the car, okay? In fact, I'd like you to leave."

He pushed himself out on my creeper. "When Benjy called, he told me about his Ass Burgers or whatever the hell it is, and I apologized to him. Which I wanted to do earlier, but I didn't have your phone number. So now I'm apologizing to both of you, okay? I ain't perfect. But I'm dealin' with stuff, and now I'm gonna really deal with it. The docs at the VA give me pills to take, and maybe now I'll take 'em, cuz what I said wasn't right. I want to make it up to you."

"It's Asperger's," corrected Benjy. "Asperger's Syndrome. People with Asperger's call each other Aspergians or Aspies sometimes. My dad is an Aspie too, but not like me. He's more like a normal."

Kenny grinned at me. "Well, ain't we a threesome?" he chuckled. "So, Big Ben, let me do you this favor and fix this."

I still didn't like him. I still wanted him gone, even if Benjy did like him. Who knew if or when he'd blow up again? And I didn't want Benjy around when he did. "Please—really—I accept your apology," I said, "but you don't have to fix the car. I screwed it up, I want to fix it."

Kenny shook his head doubtfully. "I'll tell you right now, you made a helluva mess. There's too much damage to fix for amateurs. And you don't want to go to some tire shop where you got a kid banging on it who don't know a Corvair from a can of tuna. They won't have the right wheel studs. They'll torque it all wrong. Like you did. And don't EVER ask them to align the wheels—you'll be in a World of Pain. You're gonna need a new wheel, by the way. All that wheel wobble grooved out the holes. Yeah, you did a serious number on this bad boy. You got a decent spare?"

I guess Kenny didn't appreciate the way I was looking at him. He sat up from the creeper.

"What?" he challenged. "I said I was sorry. You don't want to drive your Vair? You don't like free? You cain't forgive? Then, of the three of us, I'd say you got the biggest problem of all."

"It's okay, Dad," Benjy said.

I finally relented.

"Now, if you could please get me the spare?" Kenny ordered. "It's hard to get up off this creeper when your legs don't work."

"Don't push my ability to forgive," I shot back, as I opened the engine compartment and retrieved the spare tire. "Around our house, you better respect both of us."

Momentarily chastened, Kenny nodded. Then he asked Benjy, with a wink, "Which was it you think got him? The forgiveness or the free?"

"Probably the free," Benjy answered seriously. "He is cheap."

"Benjy," I cautioned, still steaming.

"It's true," he insisted.

"Don't talk about private family stuff with strangers."

"He's not a stranger. His name is Kenny and this is the second time we've met him."

"Look, Big Ben," said Kenny. "I'll be out of your way as soon as I'm done." He turned to Benjy. "Kid, go to the World's Coolest Car over there, please, and fetch my tool box. And the parts next to it."

"My name is Ben," I said coolly as Benjy hustled over to Kenny's rust-splotched, down-in-the-mouth Early Model. "Not Big Ben."

Kenny shrugged; he didn't care.

"Uhhhh," Benjy grunted as he lifted Kenny's tool box. "It's heavy!"

"Maybe the Ben that's bigger will help you?" Kenny said, winking at me.

I should have been amused. Instead, I just wanted him gone.

"I'm okay!" Benjy insisted. He freed the tool box and waddled over with it. "This is really, really heavy!" he complained.

"Boy, where were you when they handed out muscles?" Kenny teased.

As Benjy hustled back to Kenny's car for the parts, he noted, "Human beings all have the same number of muscles."

"I see," nodded Kenny, sending a look my way that said he was starting to understand a little more about Benjy's Ass Burgers.

"I can read the directions, if you want," offered Benjy. "I did that for my dad when we installed the seat belts."

"You installed those seat belts in the rear?" Kenny asked me.

I nodded. Proudly.

Kenny shook his head. "Good thing I'm here. You need some rust preventer to cover those bolt heads. You drill holes through the bottom of a Corvair, you're just beggin' rust to come inside and eat it for lunch."

My pride turned to cluelessness. Of course, he was right. Why hadn't I thought of it?

"That wasn't in the manual," Benjy insisted. "The manual says —"

I interrupted, telling Benjy he didn't have to recite the manual anymore.

"That's okay. Nobody's born a mechanic," said Kenny, trying hard to show he'd turned over a new leaf. "Look at the bright side, you didn't kill nobody." He giggled to himself—so much for the new leaf. "I got a spray can of rustproofing in my car we can use. It's just common sense, that's probably why they don't put it in the manual." He put a hand on the brake drum to pull himself upright. "Hand me that hammer, please, Big Guy. It's time to inflict some damage on this bad boy."

"Do you want me to read the manual to you?" Benjy again offered, eagerly handing the hammer.

"I think I got this one covered," said Kenny, maneuvering himself on the creeper. He banged the brake drum loose while schooling us on the art of replacing broken wheel lugs on a Corvair. Benjy was enthralled, concentrating hard, soaking the information in, memorizing.

With night coming fast, I watched from my office window while Benjy shouted "Bye!" and waved to Kenny as he drove off. After a few minutes of their nonstop Corvair chatter, I realized I was a third wheel. I wasn't sure they even noticed when I'd returned inside.

Annie used to say, "Any friend of Benjy's is better than no friend at all." Clearly, she had never met Kenny. Still, he had taken Benjy's mind off the catastrophe with Lydia, and I was thankful for that. And, reflecting back now, I couldn't remember the last time Benjy and I had yakked for two hours about anything, as he had just done with Kenny. And I couldn't recall the last time Benjy had waved goodbye to me without Mavis prompting him. I was jealous.

Polynomials, linear equations, factors, radicals, logarithms—I hadn't crossed paths with these terms, symbols, and formulae in decades. Once upon a time, I must have known all this stuff, because I had graduated from college and knowing it was required to enter college. (There was a mathematical term for that kind of logic, but I'd long forgotten it.) So, as Benjy prepped to take his math assessment, I was useless to him. It didn't matter, though; after weeks of taking the online tutorials, his practice assessment scores were high enough to avoid retaking the math courses he'd already passed in high school. He was ready to take the real test.

We drove the Corvair over to James Monroe, where Katie had reserved a private room in the school's Learning Center for Benjy so he would not be distracted as he took the test. She and I made certain he had all the tools he was allowed: pencils, erasers, scratch paper, and a calculator. He was eager and confident. We high-fived, then he entered the private room. He had three hours to finish the test.

An hour later, he called. He was done. "It was easy," he said. "I finished early."

As I pulled the Corvair into the James Monroe circle, he was pacing to and fro, flapping his hand and reciting.

"Congratulations," I crowed as he climbed in. "You want to celebrate?"

"No, thanks," he said dourly.

"Maybe go to the McDonald's drive-thru?" I urged, hoping he'd reconnect with Lydia.

"No, thanks," he said more dourly.

"So what was your score?" I asked as we pulled away from the school.

"It wasn't all we had hoped for," he said, repeating the very same words he'd used to inform me he'd been rejected by Wheeler.

"I thought it was easy," I said.

"So did I. When I called you, they hadn't scored the test yet."

He told me his score; it certainly wasn't "all we had hoped for." In fact, it was so bad that he now faced taking two and a half years of remedial math before he would be allowed to enroll in his one required college math course. Or, he could sign up for intensive tutoring at James Monroe, then retake the assessment. He quickly agreed to the tutoring.

"I thought I did good," he said, perplexed. Then he asked, "Dad, why do I need to know more math than you?"

"I don't know." I pulled onto the main highway and suggested we go to McDonald's, hoping to cheer him up. "We might see Lydia," I said, foregoing subtlety.

"No, thank you," said Benjy tersely.

"We could apologize again for what happened. Show her the car's fixed."

"She hates this car," he erupted. "You always tell me to pick up on the social cues! She called it a Deathmobile! Wasn't that a pretty obvious social cue?"

"Maybe we can change her mind," I said calmly. "The same way you changed your mind about this car."

"She has a boyfriend, Dad!"

"That doesn't mean she can't be your friend. I think she really likes you as a friend."

Benjy shook his head from side to side. Absolutely not.

"Okay, so what do you want to do?" I asked. "Eat lunch someplace else? Go home?"

"I want to go to Kenny's," he said.

I sighed. Loudly. Disapprovingly. He picked up that social cue right away.

"He said I should come by, he had something he wanted to show me."

"When did he say that?"

"Before he left our house."

I sighed so long that I ran out of air and coughed. The Mother of all Social Cues.

"You and Mom told me I should try to make friends," said Benjy. "I did. Kenny is my friend. I'm old enough to choose who I want to make my friend." He fixed his brown eyes on me.

I sighed again. Because he was right. I set the Corvair on a course toward Kenny's.

CHAPTER 10

As we stepped out of the Corvair, Manny, Moe, and Jack charged, barking wildly. But Benjy was prepared; he clenched his teeth, shut his eyes, and merely turned crimson, not purple. "Stop it, ya damn dogs!" Kenny yelled from the barn door. Manny, head down, suddenly quieted, looking disappointed he wouldn't be able to maul us, then led the other two hounds over to sniff us as if we were doggie treats.

"Will they jump?" Benjy anxiously called to Kenny.

"They damn well better not," Kenny threatened, which did not answer Benjy's question. He whistled, and the dogs trotted back over to him. "I guess you don't smell like a bill collector," he joked.

Benjy's face slowly gave up its crimson flush.

"Looks like yer wheel stayed on this time," Kenny needled as we joined him. I thanked him for his house call and praised his mechanical savvy, but I'm sure he also picked up on my I Don't Like You and I Don't Want to Be Here social cue.

In the garage, Kenny's Early Model was up on jack stands, its rear wheels dangling down like Humpty Dumpty's legs just before he fell. "You're working on the World's Coolest Car," Benjy said.

Kenny nodded. "That Early Model has the rear axles Nader didn't like. Said they'd make the car spin or roll." He wheeled over to the accused axles and mused, "I got history with these cars, Kid. No real problems and lotsa good times, real good times. You reminded me of that. And if I told ya about them times—" He winked toward me. "Yer Ol' Man would blow a head gasket."

"No, he wouldn't," Benjy said, wanting to hear the stories.

Kenny smiled. Since we'd met him, it was the first time I'd seen him smile, and it made him look 10 years younger, as if he could have been Benjy's older brother. "My Ol' Man and me always went deer huntin' the day the season opened," he said. "We went up to the woods at three in the mornin'. I'd skip school. I was never much for school—now I sorta wish I had been. Anyway, we went in our truck. Four-wheel drive, huge wheels and tires, practically needed a ladder to get in it. It could go anywhere. Except one year, opening day, middle of the night, and it wouldn't start. Just flat would not go."

Kenny rolled over to his dimly lit work bench, and we followed. "So Dad and me put all our huntin' stuff in the World's Coolest Car over there. Drove through mud, swamp, streams…. We beat that thing like a government mule. I bagged a twelve-point buck that day. We tied it to the Vair's roof, drove it to the check station. Man there laughed his head off, then took that picture."

From his chair, Kenny couldn't reach the back end of the bench, so I brought the framed picture to him. Yellowing and crooked inside its frame, it showed Kenny, perhaps 10 years old, the spitting image of his father beside him, standing proudly in front of their Early Model with the buck tied to the roof. Kenny choked back tears. "After that, we only hunted in Corvairs. We wuz a sight."

"Corvairs have excellent traction in mud and snow," Benjy said, "with the weight of the engine, transmission, and differential all in the rear."

Kenny nodded and handed the photo to Benjy. "I expect you prob'ly ain't hunters," he said. "Maybe it's a terrible thing to you. But that's what Dad and me did, hunted and fixed Corvairs."

Benjy noted that hunting was the primary means of food-gathering in many cultures.

"My father had a Corvair, too," I said. "He drove his carpool to work in it—four big men. They loved it because it had so much room inside."

"Roomiest compact car in the world," Kenny said.

"And economical," I added. "No antifreeze. No radiator. Easy on gas. Didn't need power steering or brakes with all the weight in back. My dad loved all that."

"Grandpa was cheap," Benjy added. "It runs in the family, like Asperger's."

Kenny slapped his thigh and cackled gleefully. "Never met a Corvair owner that wasn't tight with a dollar. Including my pa and me. But here's a secret." Benjy leaned in to hear the secret. "Don't ever call Corvair owners cheap. That offends them. They're 'frugal.'"

"I think they're smart," said Benjy.

"Oh boy," exclaimed Kenny. "You're askin' for a fight there. Most people out there think Corvair owners are dumb as door knobs."

"Those people are like the bullies on the long bus," said Benjy. "People need to accept and accommodate differences in cars and not reject or stereotype them, just like they need to accept and accommodate people with differences, and not reject or stereotype us."

"If you're runnin' for office," said Kenny, "you got my vote."

"It's not right when people call it a Deathmobile," Benjy went on. "That's what my Dad's friends called it when he was growing up."

"Deathmobile?" exclaimed Kenny. "That's funny." He gestured that we follow him to the back of the barn. "I need to show you somethin'," he said as he wheeled. "The reason I asked you to come down."

The disembodied mannequin legs lay lifeless in the dirt before the shark Corvair, just as we'd left them a few weeks earlier.

"I told ya my daddy and me, we wuz buildin' this car to race," said Kenny, his mischievous grin lifting and lighting his face. He barely looked older than Benjy now. "But I joined the Army and stuff happened and he died, so that was the end of that."

"In what kind of race do you paint your car up like a shark and pretend to have dead bodies sticking out of its mouth?" I asked.

"Well, sir," he explained, "it's a famous race in France. The Grand Prix du Gar-bahhhge," he said in a phony French accent.

Benjy drew a blank. "Garbage," I told him. "The Grand Prix of Garbage. It's a joke. A race for cars that are garbage."

"A Corvair is not garbage," Benjy insisted. "It had many innovations, such as—"

"Stop! I know!" Kenny held up his hand like a traffic cop and Benjy halted his sermon in mid-sentence. "In this race, you cain't spend more than five hundred dollars on yer car, max, other than for safety stuff—tires, brakes, safety cage and seat," Kenny explained. "And then, part of the fun of the race is everyone decorates their garbage car. So it's sort of like racing parade floats." Kenny signaled with his finger for Benjy to come close. When Benjy did, Kenny lowered his voice, sharing a secret. "We got this car for free, all we had to do was haul it away. So it's perfect for the Grand Prix, we can spend all five hundred bucks to fix it. Then we painted it up to be a killer shark. Get it? Cuz the Corvair is a killer car. Right?"

"No, I don't think so," Benjy said.

"In people's minds," I chimed in, seeing Benjy was taking Kenny too literally.

Benjy digested that, then asked Kenny, "Were you making a joke? Based on the stereotype of the Corvair as an unsafe car that was deadly?"

"Bingo," said Kenny.

Benjy solemnly nodded.

"My dad and me, we had a name for this car that we were about to paint on its side," Kenny continued. "You know what it was?"

Benjy shook his head No.

Kenny motioned to him to lean down and whispered it in his ear.

"Deathmobile?" said Benjy.

Kenny slowly nodded, then grinned mischievously.

Benjy solemnly nodded yet again.

And then he started to laugh. Big laughs. Body heaving laughs. "HA, HA, HA, HA! HA, HA, HA, HA, HA!"

Kenny slapped his thigh again and again. I thought I saw tears come to his eyes, he was laughing so hard.

"HA, HA, HA, HA! HA, HA, HA, HA, HA!" Benjy turned purple again, this time from laughter. I hadn't seen him laugh like that since Grandpa had tickled him silly.

It was contagious. I laughed at their laughing, and now we were all giggling like naughty school boys.

Benjy finally ran out of gas, laughter-wise, and sighed, "Oh, gosh...."

Usually, I had to explain jokes to him. This time, he explained the joke to me. "Deathmobile, Dad. Just like Grandpa's Corvair."

I got it. It was funny, certainly funnier than what happened next.

"So, guys," said Kenny, "the next Grand Prix is comin' up. And it ain't really in France, it's just over in West Virginia. I'm thinking it's time for me to get off my tail and race again; they said I could if I put hand controls in the car. So I'll need a race team and I'm thinkin' it should be us—Team Deathmobile. What do you say? You want to go racing?"

Benjy's eyes bulged and his jaw dropped. I thought he was about to levitate up to the barn roof.

I, on the other hand…

"I could race?" Benjy gasped. "In a real car?"

"Hell, yes! That's the point!" said Kenny. "The three of us—a team!"

"But they must require a driver's license," I said, hoping to let Benjy down easy, "and Benjy doesn't have one."

"Oh," said Kenny, deflated. "I figured you did. You're old enough."

"I can get one!" Benjy insisted.

"But will the state let you have a license?" I murmured, still trying to let Benjy down easy. "You always say they discriminate against you."

"I'm not letting them discriminate against me anymore!" Benjy roared. "I want to race!"

"Hell," Kenny unhelpfully interjected, "it ain't really even a race; the goal is just to keep a junky car rollin' to the finish. There ain't no Dale Earnhardts out there."

"Denny Hamlin is my favorite driver!" Benjy exclaimed. "He grew up in Virginia! He was Sprint Cup Rookie of the Year in 2006! And I beat him in my video game every time!"

"There ya go!" encouraged Kenny. "Sounds like yer ready to race."

"The state has some concerns about Benjy driving," I gently warned, "so it seems premature to be talking about him racing. Maybe in a year or two, but for now…"

"Heck, have you seen some of the drivers on the road lately?" Kenny interrupted, waving me off. "He can drive better than them, I'll bet. Cain't ya?"

"I want to try!" Benjy declared. "I want to race and overcome discrimination!"

"There ya go again!" Kenny shouted, raising his hand up. "Let's go race this garbage!" Benjy slapped him a high five.

I was stunned. It had been Benjy, not me, who had decided he would not try for his driver's license. He felt he was taking a principled stand against the DMV's insistence that a person with Asperger's provide medical records and undergo extra testing before being awarded the privilege of driving an automobile upon a public highway. I confess I had not tried very hard to persuade Benjy otherwise; I was just fine with his not driving an automobile. Like many with Asperger's, his reaction time was slow and his coordination poor. And what if Benjy became distracted reciting his stories to himself while he was behind the wheel? Like the DMV, I was worried about safety. I believed the DMV's cautious approach was fair.

But suddenly, that had all changed; now Benjy wanted to drive. And race. Not just in a video game, but in a real car. Yet, to put him behind the wheel on a racetrack, where concentration, skill, judgment, instinct, and reflexes would be vital, even in a race of junk cars that was just for fun—I didn't see how I could let him.

"You said you wanted to help me to live independently," Benjy fumed as we drove home and I shared my concerns. "Driving will help me live independently."

"Benjy, I'm not saying you shouldn't get your driver's license. But of course I worry about you driving, because I'm your parent and I love you, so I always worry about what could possibly happen to you. That's the way parents are."

"You said you'd help me find my own place," he said insistently.

"But, until a few minutes ago, you were adamant that you wouldn't drive because of the DMV's discrimination. What happened to that?"

"I was afraid they wouldn't let me," Benjy said, gazing out the window. "So I didn't even want to try." He turned to me. "But now I want to try. I can drive, Dad. I can do it."

What would Annie say, I wondered? She'd always been a protective parent; while the thought of Benjy driving had merely worried me, it gave her nightmares. Now would she just say no? Maybe she would, but she wasn't here anymore; I was on my own. "Benjy, I will help you try," I said. "But you'll have to demonstrate to both the state and me that you'll be a safe driver on the road, for your sake and for everyone else's. As for racing—I just don't see how anyone can race who doesn't even have a license yet."

Benjy stared straight ahead, teeth clenched. "If I try hard enough, I can do anything. Mom always said that."

Mom also said that under no circumstances should he drive an automobile, but I kept that to myself. "We'll see," I said. "But I can't promise anything."

"You should keep your eyes on the road when you drive," Benjy said, eager to demonstrate his driving knowledge. "You're missing our turn."

Too late. I'd passed the entry ramp onto the Interstate. I made an awkward U-turn, which Benjy critiqued as illegal. He was right, but we were in the middle of nowhere and there wasn't another car to be seen. Suddenly, he was becoming the World's Worst Back Seat Driver.

We traveled in silence on the Interstate. Until Benjy said, "You're driving too fast."

"I'm below the speed limit," I insisted. "The other traffic is passing us."

"It's too fast," Benjy insisted right back. "I can tell."

"Now that you want your license, you're going to give me driving lessons? I happen to be a good driver. I have never gotten a speeding ticket."

"In *Rain Man*, Raymond Babbitt was an 'excellent driver.' He said that all the time! And he was autistic. I'm only an Aspie. So I can be an excellent driver, too!"

"Benjy, you are not Raymond Babbitt. And even in the movie, Raymond did not drive out on the public highway next to other speeding drivers, he only drove up and down his driveway." A memory suddenly washed over me: standing in the children's section of the local bookstore as Benjy, age four, recited children's stories, without the book, to an audience of captivated preschoolers—and my father. One amazed parent leaned over and jokingly murmured "Rain Man" to me, not knowing I was Benjy's father. I smiled politely and said nothing. Later, I told Annie I wished I had said something. She asked me what I would have said. I didn't know, and I still don't. Just—I felt I hadn't stood up for my son. I felt like a coward.

I punched the accelerator at the memory, and the Corvair surged forward.

"You're driving too fast," Benjy declared. "The speedometer says you're speeding."

"The speedometer is not accurate," I explained. "In old cars, speedometers are often wrong." I sounded like an impatient and pedantic scold even to myself.

"You're speeding. You'll get a speeding ticket."

"Trucks are passing me!"

"They're speeding too! Two wrongs do not make a right!"

Suddenly a THUMP came from the engine in the rear and the Corvair wobbled.

"What was that?" Benjy demanded, worry in his voice.

I scanned the gauges for a clue. Nothing. Then the GEN-FAN warning light on the instrument panel meekly reared its ugly head, a faint orange glow that grew in intensity, brighter and brighter, as if slowly summoning up the courage to deliver the bad news. The TEMP-PRESS light had no such reticence—it suddenly blazed red.

I smelled trouble—intense fumes from behind me. The Corvair's air-cooled engine was quickly overheating and cooking the motor oil. I lifted my foot off the accelerator and coasted to a stop on the shoulder of the Interstate.

"I think we broke the fan belt," I sheepishly opined.

"Not 'we'—you," corrected Benjy. "I wasn't driving too fast. I wouldn't drive too fast. I would be a better driver than you. I would be an excellent driver!"

CHAPTER 11

On the shoulder of the Interstate, I hoisted the Corvair's engine lid and immediately saw the fan belt was ripped to shreds. It was a common Corvair malady, so common in fact that, when Wally had sold me the car, he had generously included a spare belt that I discovered sitting serenely in the trunk, just begging to be installed. He'd even included a wrench so that I could install it. Alas, my Corvair repair manuals were home in my garage, so I was flying blind. With wrench and belt in hand, I stared at the engine and tried to imagine how, if I were a fan belt, I would wish to be installed.

"Dad?" Benjy asked. "Do you know what you're doing?"

"Nope." Today, I would enjoy no Zen moment successfully repairing the car and resuming our trip home. Instead, I ground my teeth in frustration.

"We should call Kenny. He'll come to fix it."

Sure, Kenny was close by and could undoubtedly replace the belt in 30 seconds with his eyes closed while eating a ham sandwich. But I couldn't bear to call him. I could hear his voice ringing in my ears like tinnitus. "Man, you cain't put on a fan belt? I'll bet Benjy wouldn't be breakin' no fan belt. You oughta be lettin' him drive." Right now, I'd rather eat the fan belt than call Kenny.

"I'll call the auto club for a tow," I said. "I'll fix it at home."

"We should call a professional mechanic," Benjy said. "Kenny is a professional mechanic."

"No," I insisted, too loudly. "I'll fix it. I'll enjoy a Zen moment. Just not right now."

Naturally, the auto club sent the very same tow truck operator who came when the wheel nearly broke off. He pulled up in front of our marooned Corvair, its trunk lid raised forlornly and heat waves still rising off its engine, and hopped out sporting a grin that was miles too wide. "Told ya you'd be callin'," he grinned.

I had not grinned back. As we once again rode home in the cab of the wrecker, I wondered what made my dad such a Corvair fan. What inspired such a sober and judicious man to not merely drive such an unconventional car, but to sing hosannas, wax rhapsodic, proselytize other sober and judicious men about the virtues of joining him in the Corvair Brotherhood? Why would he good-naturedly suffer the slings and arrows launched his way from my friends, and likely his friends too, because of his stubborn devotion to this car that was taking over my life?

Don't get me wrong, I did enjoy driving my Corvair. I loved that its big booty made it so sure-footed around curves and turns. I delighted in hearing perfect strangers' Corvair stories. I appreciated that the car was a hugely risky attempt by a risk-averse giant American corporation to rethink the automobile—to start over again with a clean sheet of paper and build the smartest, most efficient mass-market compact car that it possibly could imagine. Even as the wrecker again lowered it ignominiously onto my driveway, I marveled at its beautiful slipstream shape, still fresh and sexy, coiled to lunge forward like a jungle cat, even as it sat broken. And that was the point; it was broken. Again. Instead of giving me a Zen-like satisfaction as I solved its mechanical issues and kept it humming along the road, it was starting to drive me nuts.

To my father, I knew the Corvair had been more than a mere car. It was a symbol of something, a declaration about himself; he was a Company Man, yes, but that would not define him. He had intellectual curiosity and wasn't afraid of quirkiness and nonconformity. He was a free thinker. He wasn't afraid to take a chance on something different. But why wasn't I feeling all that right now? What wasn't I getting about this car? Why wasn't I feeling the love?

Perhaps my father, usually such a cautious and sober man, bit hook, line, and sinker on GM's hugely successful campaign to introduce the Corvair in the fall of 1959 as an American car that broke the mold, eschewing the rocket fins, bosom bumpers, gas-guzzling over-powered engines, and cartoonish bloat that characterized so many of Detroit's designs of that era. Instead, this radical departure from conventional American auto making filled a niche that American car makers had forgotten about. By offering economical and comfortable performance— no more, no less—it was a new kind of car: basic transportation for the Thinking Man.

And that was my father; a Thinking Man. On the October 5, 1959, cover of *Time*, a magazine my father read devoutly from cover to cover the instant he picked it up from our mailbox, was not GM's CEO, as might be expected, but Edward N. Cole, the several-rungs-down-the-corporate-ladder general manager of the Chevrolet Division, known as the "Father of the Corvair." A Steven Jobs of his time who also played a starring role in the development of the Corvette, the catalytic converter, airbags, the famed Chevy small block V-8, and numerous other auto industry innovations, the legendary Cole had taken note of the increasing popularity of the imported Volkswagen Beetle and realized there was a huge, untapped demand for an American-style "people's car." Said the "folksy, brilliant" Cole then, "If I felt any better about our Chevy Corvair, I think I'd blow up." But of course he said that! He was the Corvair's Father! Selling Corvairs was his job! How could a sober and judicious guy like my father fall for such obvious puffery?

It turned out that Dad wasn't the only one bowled over by the new Corvair. Gushed that over-the-moon issue of *Time*: "No sooner had Chevrolet announced the Corvair than it began to write orders. Hertz Rent-a-Car signed up for 3,000. Chicago Dealer Zollie Frank wanted 10,000, but Chevy turned him down to spread the supply." In St. Louis, Chevy Dealer Gene Jantzen, located directly across from a GM factory, claimed, "People toured that plant and peeked through the knotholes at the Corvair. Some even climbed atop their cars outside the plant to get a look. Then they came over to our place and ordered a Corvair." Today, think the shivering mob queued up at the Apple Store to buy that company's latest electronic must-have wonder device.

Dad placed one of GM's first orders for a Corvair back in 1959. I was too young to have any memory of him bringing that car home. But I did cherish its cozy shelf behind the back seat, just above the warmth, hum, and vibration of the engine immediately beneath it. What a perfect crib for me to sleep in on long trips, back in the days before child safety seats.

But, five years later, I was certainly old enough to remember The Day the First Corvair Died. On our way home from church, straining to go up our steep hill, that beloved 1960 Early Model suddenly screeched to a halt, scaring the bejesus out of me far more effectively than the fire-and-brimstone sermon I'd just heard. Cautiously getting out of the car in our Sunday best, we found the car's engine had dropped out of the car and was sitting on our street. As our neighbors gathered to console us, Dad kneeled down to the air-cooled power plant, stunned. The motor mounts had broken, a Year One design flaw that was fixed in subsequent years.

Such a calamity might have caused some men to reconsider their love affair with a car. My father was not one of those men. The very next day, he brought home a brand spanking new 1965 Late Model, with the hot international look and a new and improved non-Deathmobile rear suspension. What he couldn't know was that this new Corvair, which he cherished even more than the first one, was doomed to extinction. Just a few months earlier, Ford had released the iconic, sporty, super-selling Mustang. Just a few months later, Ralph Nader published *Unsafe at Any Speed*. This one-two punch sealed the Corvair's fate. Sales dropped precipitously, then practically stopped. To battle the Mustang in the marketplace, Chevrolet introduced the front-engine, rear-drive, water-cooled Camaro. Still, General Motors, then the world's largest corporation, proud and stubborn, refused to totally abandon the Corvair. Despite losing money on each one it built, it kept the car in production three years longer than originally planned, even going so far as to build the car by hand in 1969, its final year, at a huge loss per car, just to emphatically underscore that it gave no credence to Nader's charges of corporate irresponsibility and would not bow to intense public pressure to stop selling the car.

Nor did my father abandon his Corvair. He kept ours running

longer than any other car he owned. He wanted me to drive it; I even got a few driving lessons in it. But then, one night while it was parked at the curb in front of our house, a drunken neighbor smashed into it. On hearing the crash, my father raced out of the house. I wasn't far behind. Fortunately, the neighbor was not seriously injured. But the Corvair was. It had one innovation that worked against it that night: It was one of the first American cars built utilizing "unibody" construction; like nearly all cars today, it had no rigid frame, an innovation that reduced weight and increased gas mileage. Even though the damage appeared repairable, it was not. Our beautiful blue Late Model was no more. And not even for a Corvair would my father violate his first rule of car ownership—never buy used, you were just buying someone else's problem. For our family, the Age of the Corvair was over.

That is, until I bought the Corvair that now rested in my driveway, broken, a piece of non-functional yard sculpture. As the car sat un-drivable, I gave it a wide berth, as though it were a grizzly bear that hadn't eaten in a month. Installing a new fan belt was one of the simplest Corvair repairs. Heck, it was almost as simple as rotating the tires. Which, of course, I'd botched. That failure haunted me; I could still hear Lydia crying "Deathmobile." All that psychic satisfaction I'd expected to feel working with my own two hands to repair the Vair? All I was feeling now was buyer's remorse. I could barely take a step toward the thing. It depressed me. I stayed inside just to avoid it.

"Dad?" Benjy asked. I was staring at the car through the kitchen window.

"Uh huh." Nearly a week had passed since the fan belt broke.

"When are we going to fix the car?"

"I have a lot of work. Got to get a technical manual out to a client. Tight deadline."

"Can't I call Kenny?"

"No. I'll fix the car."

"When?"

"Soon," I sighed. "I'm just not ready yet."

"I read the repair manual. It's a well-written repair manual."

"I agree. Clear, concise, well-illustrated. Definite pride of authorship. I tip my professional hat to whoever wrote it."

"Since it's so good, it makes replacing the fan belt easy."

"Do you want to try to replace it?"

"I'm not a mechanic."

"That makes two of us."

Since the belt had broken, we had replayed this same conversation at least once a day. But this time, Benjy changed subjects. "Can we go to the DMV? I'm ready to take the written test."

"What about your homework?" I muttered. "What about preparing for your math assessment?"

"My homework's done. And after I take the test at the DMV, I can go to James Monroe for more math tutoring. And then we'll come home and fix the Corvair."

"In a few days," I murmured.

"But the race is only two months away. I have to have my learner's permit for at least one month before I can apply for a driver's license. I have to have a driver's license to race. Which means we need to get to the DMV."

"That's very good math," I said. "You should do well on your assessment." Driver's license, racing, Corvair repair—it was too much. I returned to my office and pulled my work up over my head to escape.

A few days later, I could resist Benjy no longer and took him to the Department of Motor Vehicles. As we waited our turn in line, he was wired and eager to take the test, which meant that he flapped his hand like he was playing the piano one handed. He also recited some of his favorite scenes from *National Treasure*, debating with himself whether Riley was Irish or not. The attendant noticed and scrutinized him carefully. "If the applicant has any medical issues, physical or mental," she explained pointedly once we reached her desk, "those need to be disclosed on the application. A doctor will need to complete a Customer Medical Report and submit it for DMV review. Once that review is complete, the applicant will be notified if he or she is eligible take the written test for a learner's permit." The medical review could take anywhere from 10 days to several months.

"Dad, I need to have my license in two months so I can race," Benjy said urgently once we were back in the Toyota. "We need to submit the medical report."

"We'll visit Dr. Stan as soon as he can see us," I assured Benjy. But I no longer had to worry about Benjy racing; even if we saw Dr. Stan tomorrow, there was no way a legendarily unhurried bureaucracy like the DMV could review Benjy's medical records quickly enough for him to get his license in time for the race. I rarely had thought of the DMV with gratitude, but now I did; they would be the Bad Guy who denied Benjy his dream of racing—not me.

The first time I'd been in Stan Pollard's waiting room, I squeezed Annie's hand so tight that I bruised it. We sat on the sofa watching Benjy march back and forth before the unlighted fireplace, reciting the story of Thomas the Tank Engine, and James, and Percy, and the other engines on the Island of Sodor. What was wrong with a three-year-old doing this, I wondered? Why did the head of his school suggest we have him evaluated? Wasn't this a good thing, even a blessing? Wasn't it a sign of genius? So what if he didn't play with other children?

"Benjy," I'd interrupted, pointing to the portrait over the mantel. "Know who that is?"

"Mister Jefferson!" Benjy pronounced gleefully. In our slice of Virginia, where Thomas Jefferson had lived and built his two magnificent architectural masterpieces, Monticello and the University of Virginia, his portrait hung everywhere, even at McDonald's. Benjy knew Jefferson's mug by heart—and that all locals respectfully called him "Mister."

"Goodness!" said the astonished receptionist. "What a bright young man!"

"See?" I whispered to Annie. "What was wrong with that? What could be wrong?"

Clean-cut and thin as a coffee stirrer, Dr. Stanley Pollard bounded out of his office to greet us. The doc's baby face made him look like Doogie Howser, M.D.'s younger brother. "Call me Stan," he insisted. I squeezed Annie's hand even tighter—tourniquet tight. He was so young! Too young! But we had no choice; he was new in town, just starting his practice, and thus was the only child psychiatrist within an hour's drive who could see us.

Stan asked Benjy to play with blocks and other toys, and watched closely when he didn't. Stan asked him questions about Thomas the Tank Engine, and Milo and Otis. He did a few other tests, I'm sure, but by then I couldn't see out of my welled-up eyes. Suddenly, the sound of every locomotive on the Island of Sodor roared through my ears, because I could see from Stan's baby face that he knew Benjy was very different from other children. And that difference was so different that it would have a name—a diagnosis.

Stan told us about Asperger's and how it was often passed through the male parent's line. I thought of my own issues with socializing and obsession. I recalled decades earlier overhearing my father tell a friend that I "march to the beat of a different drummer." I remembered my mother urging me to "go out and play. Make friends. Stop living in your own little world."

We would eventually get a confirming second opinion. But before we even left Stan's office, I knew he was right. And so did Annie. In a way, it was a relief. It explained so much. And it wasn't as if Asperger's was something that no one had ever dealt with before. It was not a tragedy, and not a cause for mourning. Rather, it was a difference. And it would cause our family to embark on a life's journey unlike anything we'd envisioned.

Stan ended my reverie as he emerged from his office with Benjy and said to me, "Your turn, Ben. Come on in." This was odd; I rarely got a turn of my own with Stan. Inside his office, he guided me to a chair. Now, more than a decade and a half after we first met him, he was graying. He wasn't Doogie Howser's kid brother anymore. "I just thought I'd check in with you," he began. "See how life is without Annie."

"Hard," I said. Duh.

"You miss her a lot, I know. Do you get out at all?"

"Benjy and I go for drives in the Corvair. When it runs. Which isn't all that often these days. That's about it."

"He couldn't stop talking about it," Stan grinned. "He really likes that car."

"That makes one of us," I grumbled. "It's sitting in my driveway, broken. And it got us involved with this character...." I paused to find words to describe Kenny without sounding too judgmental. "He's a vet. Disabled. I wish I could like him, I really do. But between the beer, and the tobacco chewing, and the hunting, and the hounds, and the language, and the way he mocked Benjy one day—he's not exactly a role model."

"Kenny?"

"Kenny," I affirmed, exhaling a highly judgmental sigh.

"Benjy told me a lot about Kenny. He made a friend. That's always been a goal, to make friends."

"But of all the people to make friends with—! And he's invited Benjy to drive in a car race. That's why we're here, because now Benjy wants his driver's license. And I'm terrified. So if you want to write in your report that he should never drive, that's just fine by me."

"Well, I'll tell you what I am going to write," said Stan. "I'm going to write that, with his Asperger's, Benjy's reaction time and coordination may be slower than some. But that will certainly be more than compensated for by his intense focus on being a safe driver and following the rules of the road, which he'll memorize and know by heart and never knowingly violate. He'll never joyride, and he'll never speed or use a cell phone or text while driving because that's against the rules and he will always follow the rules to the letter. In my professional opinion, he'll be one of the safest drivers on the road, certainly safer than almost any other teenager out there. What do you think of that?"

"I think I'd like a second opinion," I scowled.

Stan smiled, then got serious. "He's growing up, Ben. He wants to find his own way. His own place in a world that isn't made for him."

"I know. He tells me that a lot."

"And that's a good thing, a very good thing." Stan stretched his legs. The old Nikes he once wore had long ago been replaced by $300 walking shoes. I'd probably paid for those shoes, thanks to the lousy mental health coverage in our insurance plan. But he was worth it. Benjy loved him. So did I.

"You don't want to see him leave the nest?" Stan probed.

"Yes, I do. But the problem is that, when Annie and I talked about Benjy living independently, Annie was there. Benjy was always Annie's department. She was great with him—so patient and understanding and intuitive—and I'm not any of those things, because I'm obsessive, compulsive, and have a dash of Asperger's myself, probably. But now Benjy is my department and I'm afraid I'll screw it all up."

"You're not giving him or you enough credit. Look, Ben, lots of kids have challenges when they grow up. Lots of parents go through what you're going through. He's a responsible young man, more responsible than most that come through this office. It's just that he's so different from the crowd."

I sighed. "But what if he leaves the nest and his wings don't open? What if one of his differences ends up causing an accident? I can't be irresponsible. I can't let him or Annie down. I can't lose him, Stan, I just can't."

"In my professional medical opinion, I think he can drive safely," Stan said. "So you're not being irresponsible. But are there guarantees in life? No. Look at what happened to Annie. How many millions get the flu and don't die? Yet she did. There are no guarantees."

"That's not a reason to let him drive. It's a reason to not let him drive."

"I think he can drive safely. It's the other drivers I worry about."

I slowly conceded. "If the state believes it's safe for Benjy to drive, who am I to question? But racing? Right after he gets his license?" I shook my head and sighed.

"He told me it's not really a race," Stan said. "It sounds more like a fast parade of junkers and clunkers."

"It's enough of a race that it scares me."

"Then tell him that, in your opinion, he shouldn't race. You're his parent, it's your prerogative to say it. But he's become old enough to make his own decisions. Some of those decisions will be great and some will be less great. Just like any other young adult."

I sighed again. Loudly. "His goals and ambitions get bigger and bigger at the same time that he's losing the support and accommodations he had as a child. He desperately wants to find 'his own place,' and I just can't see it. I worry a big fat Reality Check is coming, and it'll devastate him."

"In our sessions, when Benjy talks about finding his own place, he doesn't just mean a place to live away from home. It's broader than that. It's that place in this world where he is comfortable, and accepted, and fulfilled, and secure. And Reality Checks are part of finding that place for all kids, not just Benjy. Kids who dream about becoming president or an astronaut are most likely not going to have those dreams come true. Maybe, after a year or two at community college, Benjy's place will be Wheeler. Maybe it will be his own apartment. Maybe it will be a group home. Maybe you'll convert your garage to an apartment for him. It could be anything. But there is a special place out there that will fit him, and I believe he'll find it."

"I hope so," I said, without conviction.

"You don't believe it?" Stan prodded. "Or you don't want it?"

"I never thought I'd say this, but I'll miss talking about whether Riley is Irish, or listening to Denny Hamlin lose to the greatest rookie driver in the history of NASCAR, or answering whether the envelope came or not. It all drives me up the wall sometimes. But I'd miss it. I'd miss him. I don't think I really do want him to go."

"Benjy will find his place," Stan smiled. "And you will find yours."

The next morning, I woke with a start. There was too much silence. For the first day in years, the booming bass from Benjy's racing game wasn't rattling the bedposts.

I hopped out of bed and looked inside Benjy's open bedroom door; he was gone. I took the stairs two at a time and checked the TV room. His video game rocker sat empty. The front door to the house was open. I rushed over, and then I heard through the screen door the familiar drama: *For every rookie driver, there's a first time for everything. This was Benjy Bennett's first time to try and keep from dying at Talladega. He was now driving a bucking bronco that insisted on turning right, toward the outside wall, wrecking both Hamlin and himself.*

He sat behind the wheel of the Corvair, his hands in racing position.

He imagined himself driving a bucking bronco. Trying to keep from dying.

"Take your time, DMV," I thought. "Take your own sweet bureaucratic time."

CHAPTER 12

"What the hell you drivin' that unsafe, recalled, boring piece of un-American, rice-burning trash from the people who bombed us at Pearl Harbor for?" Kenny demanded to know. "I ought to kick you off my land. Get yourself a safe car—like a Corvair! Oh wait, you already got a Corvair!" He cackled with glee.

I cringed. "Kenny," I asked, "do you have to say that in front of my son? He can't always tell when you're joking."

"I ain't joking," Kenny said.

"I'm fine," Benjy said. "I think we should just do our work."

At Benjy's insistence, we'd come to Kenny's to prepare the Deathmobile for the Grand Prix. The late spring sun beat down hot as August. Manny, Moe, and Jack were sniffing and licking me like I was dinner. One of Kenny's neighbors had just spread poultry manure on his field. As my sinuses imploded, felled by the pungent stench of roasting chicken poo, and I contemplated spending the next few hours with Kenny, the thought occurred to me that I'd rather be elsewhere.

"After we left here the last time, my dad broke the Corvair's fan belt, and now he's afraid to try to replace it," Benjy shared with Kenny. Now, with Kenny certain to tease me over my mechanical ineptitude, I was sure I'd rather be elsewhere.

"Fan belt's no harder to change than a tire!" Kenny cackled some more. "Oops, well, I see your point, given the tire problem you had." He chastised me for not laughing hard enough. "C'mon, Big Ben, it's fun! Lighten up a little! To learn, ya gotta make mistakes. Right?"

"Things are a little tense between the Corvair and me," I said, tensely. "I've put it to the side. I wish you would too."

Kenny got my hint and backed off the teasing. "Wait'll ya see this, you're gonna flip," he said, rolling himself toward the barn. Benjy offered to push him, and Kenny accepted. The barn was mercifully cooler, but the chicken poo pungency had drifted in. Kenny directed Benjy to push him all the way to the rear, then proudly asked, "Whaddya think?"

"Deathmobile" in jet black graffiti lettering had been spray-painted across the side of the shark Corvair. "We'll look so awesome, them other cars may just pull off the track and gawk at our awesomeness," Kenny cackled.

He held up his hand, and Benjy high-fived it. "Yes!" he grinned. "The New Deathmobile!"

I laughed. It was fun. But it was time to pour some necessary cold water on their parade, which seemed doomed to disappointment. "Kenny, there's still a problem," I warned. "Benjy will probably not have his driver's license in time for the race." I told him that, even if the state approved Benjy to drive, he still wasn't eligible for a driver's license until he'd had a learner's 30 days.

"That's cuttin' it close," said Kenny. "Real close." He slammed the armrest of his chair. "Shoot."

"Sorry," said Benjy.

"Not your fault," assured Kenny. "You got nothin' to be sorry for." He sighed. "I'm lookin' forward to it, that's all. I haven't been out on the track for so long. Haven't seen my friends. I've been so out of it." His cackle gave way to a deflated scowl. "So do we keep working on the car or do we sit around?"

"We work on the car!" Benjy exclaimed. "Because I should be able to drive under the Americans with Disabilities Act! We can go to court to fight this discrimination! We—"

Kenny held up his hand—Stop!—and Benjy stopped talking on a dime. "If we're plannin' on racin', then, like you said, we got work to do," he growled, wheeling to the rear of the Deathmobile. "I dropped the engine and started tearing it down. Got the pistons out. Get them for me over on the bench, if you don't mind, Big Guy."

Benjy strode ahead, pulled some engine parts off the bench, and brought them to Kenny.

"How'd you know those are the pistons?" Kenny asked, impressed. I wondered the same thing.

"I read the parts catalogs my dad has," Benjy said. "Are you rebuilding the engine?"

"Yes, sort of—doing as much as we can afford on our budget."

"To rebuild the engine, you must remember that all Corvairs are over forty years old," Benjy said, reciting from memory the guidance he'd read in one of the catalogs. "It is important to consider replacing the pistons and cylinder units in a Corvair engine because they are air-cooled. The higher operating temperatures are hard on the aluminum pistons. You should never replace just one piston. If one is bad, the others soon will be. So you should replace all of them on the same side of the engine at the same time. You should also consider new cylinder barrels. Honing and re-ringing will not remedy excessive clearance. Installing an overbore kit, containing new pistons and new precision barrels, is the proper way to address these problems and ensure a successful engine rebuilding project."

Astonished, Kenny eyed Benjy, then me. I shrugged, having witnessed Benjy's amazing recall so often. "Wow," Kenny finally said. "You're a walking, talking Corvair manual. What else?"

"We recommend that engines with over one hundred thousand miles also get a reground crankshaft and camshaft," Benjy added.

Kenny looked to me, then back to Benjy. "Who is 'we'? Not your dad. He cain't even fix a broken fan belt."

"The company that published the catalog?" I asked Benjy. He nodded yes.

Kenny eyed Benjy. "Did you just read the catalog and memorize it? Or do you know how an engine actually works?"

"When I was four, I had a computer program called 'How Things Work.' It showed how an engine actually works."

"Abso-freaking-lootly amazing," Kenny said.

"I can remember really well," said Benjy proudly.

"The curious cat and pug nose pup," I quietly sang, grinning.

"*Milo and Otis* was a long time ago, Dad!" said Benjy, annoyed as he recognized the movie's theme song. "I haven't recited that since I was six!"

Kenny shook his head in wonder, then got down to business. "Well, for the race, we can forget any kind of major rebuild. That would eat up our five-hundred-dollar Garbage budget, and leave nothing for the automatic transmission problems. So we'll have to scrounge in these boxes for parts or get them out of one of the cars out back. What do you say to that, Professor Corvair?"

"When a major engine rebuild is not practical," said Professor Corvair, not missing a beat, "we recommend a complete set of gaskets for the O-rings, oil pan, top covers, bell housing, oil pump cover, and oil cooler. It also includes all the other seals and gaskets needed. A new set of gaskets will prevent most oil leaks and increase engine performance."

"Yes! Exactly! That is abso-freaking-lootly AMAZING!" Kenny shouted. "That's exactly right! The biggest bang for the fewest bucks! Now, what do you know about tools?"

"Not much," said Benjy.

"It doesn't matter—I can teach you." Kenny was ecstatic. "Man, could I ever use you! Holy cow! You could fetch my tools, hold wrenches, tell me the repair instructions in the technical manuals. You could be my legs! The top floor's empty in my house. When can you move in?"

I cringed. Yet again. Benjy live and work here? With Kenny? Was he joking? My heart stopped, fearing Benjy would take Kenny seriously.

"No, thank you," said Benjy politely.

My heart started pumping again. Whew. Annie, we dodged a bullet there.

"We could be Professor and Doctor Corvair," Kenny joked.

"After I graduate from high school, I'm going to college," Benjy said. "To James Monroe Community College. My grandfather wanted me to go to Dartmouth, but—"

"Whatever!" Kenny interrupted impatiently. "We'll just wrench on this job. But it's pretty darn dry out there for kids comin' out of college. That's why I went in the Army. And it's even worse now with the economy so bad. But a good mechanic can always find work."

"I am going to college," Benjy said firmly. "It's part of my plan."

"Speaking of college," I said, hoping we could flee Kenny, the Deathmobile, and the roasting chicken poo, "you've got your math assessment coming up. And the way the DMV works, it's doubtful you'll be able to race. Maybe studying would be a better use of your time right now."

He looked down. Disappointed. Still, he nodded. He understood.

Suddenly, I recalled all the times on the schoolyard when he stood to the side, looking on enviously, as the other kids played ball. Or, more recently, when his teachers had assigned group work in his classes and he'd been mysteriously left out of the groups. Now he'd actually been invited to participate and utilize his unique talents. By a friend he had made. I relented. "You know what," I said. "You're a responsible guy. It's your choice."

"I've almost finished the math tutorial," he said. "I know it really well now."

"Well, then, let's stay. Abso-freaking-lootly."

He smiled a huge, very surprised smile. I loved that smile. He deserved to smile. He said he knew the math. Everything would be fine.

"Did the envelope from the DMV come today?" Benjy asked.

Barely a hundred hours had passed since we'd seen Doc Pollard, I reminded him. As he did with the envelope from Wheeler, he would ask every day whether the DMV envelope had come.

With Benjy's senior year at high school wrapping up, ebullient Katie in the James Monroe Disability Office sent me an e-mail urging that Benjy retake his math assessment as soon as possible; fall college registration was well underway and she didn't want him to be shut out of a class he needed. I explained to her that, for hours each day, Benjy concentrated hard on the math tutorial. He had no choice; I'd spent those hours with him, looming over his shoulder, then catching up on my own work after he'd fallen asleep. When his mind wandered to Corvairs, or racing Denny Hamlin, or Lydia, or *National Treasure,* or elsewhere, I cleared my throat. My throat was on fire, I told her. She replied to my joke with a line of smiling and dancing emoticons, then a series of questions about Benjy and his Asperger's, and asked for my suggestions on how she could best ensure his success at college.

I told her that the best thing she could do for Benjy was get James Monroe to waive its math requirement. I wanted her to know that, for Benjy, math was hieroglyphics, and he didn't have a Rosetta Stone to help him translate. His weakness in math was likely my fault, I told her. Until I discovered my mobile phone had a calculator, I asked waitresses how much I should tip them. No wonder they fought to have me seated at their tables. In her reply to that joke, Katie sent me guffawing emoticons, then sweetly informed me there was no waiving Benjy's math requirement, and asked if I knew what made math so hard for him.

Benjy might know how to do the math, I wrote back, but where he often struggled was in understanding what he was being asked. Key words, clues, and concepts in word problems often threw him for a loop, or else caused him to ask questions rather than give answers. If a test asked, "Did the seller earn a profit?" Benjy might stop and consider: Was a profit only money? What if the seller liked selling so much that he'd do it for free? Or he just happened to like the buyer? Should that count as "profit"? Benjy also disdained scratch paper and calculators, even if the test suggested he use them. It was a point of pride for him; he wanted to work everything out in his head. But then, in the middle of working a problem, his mind might shift tracks and focus on things that interested him more, like the ever-fascinating conundrum of why Riley was called Irish in *National Treasure*. After a few minutes of puzzling through that riddle, the math problem was a distant memory and he had to start the problem all over again.

Katie e-mailed me a list of test-taking techniques she thought might be helpful. She suggested that Benjy slowly say the test questions out loud, word by word, to make sure he understood them before trying to answer, and to block other thoughts from distracting him. He should have a rule to use the calculator for every computation—no exceptions!—even if the problem was as simple as two plus two. He should employ the process of elimination, crossing out wrong answers to multiple-choice questions and then choosing an answer from the ones remaining. He should check over the answers a second and third time.

Of course! A list! Just like Annie would have made! What hadn't I thought of that? After I had Benjy follow the list, his practice scores improved dramatically, I e-mailed Katie. I also told her about Annie and her lists, and a lot of other stuff about Annie that, an instant after I hit the Send button, I realized was far too personal. What possessed me to do that? Was that ordinary social awkwardness or Asperger's? Or loneliness? Whichever, she wrote back quickly, this time with lots of Thumbs Up emoticons, and suggested Benjy retake the assessment the next Saturday. And she talked about how great Annie was and how hard it must have been to lose her. She said it just right: not too much empathy, but not too little. I admired that so much. I admired that she e-mailed me so often and replied back to me so quickly. And that she liked my jokes. And she had such gorgeous teeth.

On Saturday morning, I prepared Benjy a lighter breakfast than usual; getting him too full might make him drowsy. During one math test he took after lunch a few years earlier, he'd put his head on his desk and napped. As he ate toast with jam from one hand, he paced intensely, reciting, "Principal. Interest. Compound interest. Amortization," while flapping his other hand to the cadence of each syllable. He knew this stuff cold.

We made our way across the driveway to the Toyota and he stopped reciting to say, "Dad, we need to fix the Corvair. The fan belt is one of the easiest—"

"Focus," I interrupted. "No distractions."

"Right!" he agreed. "No distractions! Remember Katie's list!"

At the Learning Center, as the attendant prepared the private test-taking room reserved for Benjy, I asked if Katie was going to meet us. "It's Saturday, Dad," Benjy said, eyeing me closely. "She doesn't have a job like yours. Lots of people don't work on Saturday." The attendant confirmed it, and also said that Benjy was not allowed to take her list into the test-taking room.

"Possibly it would have been helpful to you if Katie could go over her test-taking techniques with you one last time," I said. "So I'm disappointed she's not here, that's all."

Benjy eyed me even more closely. He wasn't usually adept at reading the subtext of a conversation. But he saw one here.

"I know how to take the test," he assured me. As he closed the door to the test-taking room, he said, "You just like to see her teeth."

Three hours later, I waited in the Camry at James Monroe's front door. When Benjy emerged, he marched to the car as he always did, betraying nothing.

"So? How'd it go?" I asked as he opened the car door.

"Fine," he said.

"Did they give you a score?"

"Yes." I waited. He waited. Then he finally repeated the words I hoped never to hear again: "It wasn't all that we'd hoped for."

His score was worse than the first time he took the test.

"I wasn't allowed to take Katie's list in," he explained.

"But you had memorized it," I said. "You didn't need the actual piece of paper the list was written on, did you?"

"It wasn't the same," he said.

I winced. I sighed. I was bewildered. How could Benjy put in dozens of hours on the tutorial and have his score actually decline? Now he still faced two and a half years of remedial math before he could take the college-level math course required to graduate.

"I can do better," he said. "I know I can."

I couldn't be angry. He had worked hard, and somehow that just hadn't registered on the test. We'd figure something out. I rubbed his shoulders. He leaned forward so I'd scratch the center of his back.

"Dad, did the envelope from the DMV come yet?" he asked.

It hadn't come.

After the test, Benjy wanted to drive to Kenny's. They worked together on the engine rebuild, Benjy handing Kenny the tools and parts as he repeated the instructions over and over, whether Kenny wanted to hear them or not. I excused myself and went outside, where the chicken poo pungency was fortunately no more. Wandering, I found myself drawn to the rusting Corvairs in Kenny's back field. No one had ever answered Kenny's Craigslist plea to come to their rescue, so they were destined for the scrap yard. It was an ignominious end to a celebrated experiment in automotive innovation. But what other fate could there be for a car that was now best known as a failure, a botch job, a punch line, a menace to society, a killer, and the car that even a half-century later was still being blamed for bankrupting General Motors? No matter how unfair that fate might be, how could the Corvair not be shunned and voted off the American island?

Yet, the Corvair still had its fans and friends. And they had stubbornly kept them in fields like Kenny's all over the country, resisting sending them to the scrap yard for recycling. In Gettysburg, Pennsylvania, a musket-shot away from our nation's greatest battlefield, the Corvair Ranch gave refuge to more than 700 Corvairs that over the years would give up a useful part here or piece of bodywork there to a Vair that still endured. But here in Kenny's field, these Corvairs couldn't even look forward to those meager prospects. They endured their fate in stoic dignity, peacefully rusting, awaiting one final journey down the highway—the highway to the crusher.

I stopped as I realized I was making the same connection Benjy had—that the Corvair was a different car that he, a different boy, could identify with and appreciate. But now in this field I confronted the fate the different Corvair faced in our society; having so much life still to give, they instead sat here decomposing in the muck because the world had no place for them. How could I make sure my different son did not suffer the same fate? How could he find his own satisfying and accepting place in the world?

I didn't know. All I knew was I had to get away from these Corvairs, and quickly returned to the barn.

CHAPTER 13

Sitting alone in the bleachers in Benjy's high school gymnasium, I used up all my Kleenex as he accepted a Senior Day award as the school's Most Outstanding Special Ed Student. All his accomplishments were recounted: the autism and disability panels and workshops he'd participated in, the novel he'd written, the plays he'd performed in, the volunteer work he'd done. As Benjy dutifully strode to the podium to accept his award, I read amazement on more than a few parents' faces. For his hand-flapping, pacing, and self-talking, Benjy was one of the most recognized students at the school. Many didn't know there was much more to this book than its cover.

The academic departments handed out their awards next. As I settled back to applaud Benjy's classmates, I wondered how he felt right now. His successes usually had "special" or "disability" pinned to them, and that frosted him. He said it was like being told, "You're great, considering how abnormal you are." Judging by how unimpressed he'd looked as he accepted today's award, I expected he'd probably dismiss it as just another left-handed compliment. I'd have to speak to him about that. He should be proud that he had achieved so much. He shouldn't feel like a second-class citizen.

Suddenly, my ears perked up. Ms. Burnley, Benjy's English teacher, his favorite, was speaking. "I've had the pleasure of getting to know this student and his writing over the past two years in my Creative Writing class. As a writer, he authored his own novel, displaying and developing a strong, confident voice...."

Wait. What? Was there some student at this school other than Benjy who authored a novel?

"This student's questioning mind and passion for learning will no doubt bring him great success in the years ahead…."

Annie, are you listening to this? Can you hear? Can you believe it?

"He's a wonderful role model for his peers. The English Department's Most Outstanding Student Award goes to Benjamin Bennett the Third."

Benjy again mounted the podium, this time with his most surprised and enthusiastic grin. As if they could read his overjoyed mind, the parents and students this time rose in a standing ovation. Kleenex came at me from every side to sponge up my uncontrollable blubbering. Benjy got a warm embrace from Ms. Burnley, then waved shyly to the crowd.

Oh Annie, I hope you are seeing this.

All his grumbling about the disability asterisk on his achievements? Not this time. That talk I had to have with him about thinking he was a second-class citizen? Never mind.

When I caught up to Benjy after the ceremony, I reached out to hug him, but he resisted; like many kids with Asperger's, he wasn't wild about hugging or touching. So I raised my hand high and he high-fived it gingerly. "You are the Toast of the School," I declared. "We are celebrating."

"Thanks," Benjy said, grudgingly. He was never one for compliments. Besides, right now, I could see, his thoughts were elsewhere. Far down the hall, Lydia was surrounded by friends.

"Go on," I nudged. "Say hello. I'll bet she wants to congratulate you on your award."

"She's with her friends, Dad!" Benjy protested.

"You're her friend, too. And you are The Man today. You are Big Man on Campus. Go up to her."

Benjy thought about it. He took a step. Lydia saw him and waved. He took another step.

And then Lydia's boyfriend planted a big fat kiss on her lips that went on and on and on.

"Let's go home," Benjy said, deflated.

"C'mon," I urged. "The kiss will end, and then you can talk."

"No," he insisted. "I want to go home and see if the envelope came."

I dropped Benjy off at the curb to grab the mail, then pulled the Camry into the driveway. I saw his head drop after he'd thumbed through the stack. Clearly, the DMV envelope hadn't come. "Dad," he said as he pulled himself despondently up the drive, "it's only thirty-three days till the race."

"Maybe we should tell the DMV about these great awards you just got," I said. "Maybe they can put a hurry on it."

"They aren't for driving, Dad!" he said, throwing up his hands.

"But they are for character and intelligence and responsibility and focus. Those should all be important to them in deciding whether you can drive." I was just trying to cheer Benjy up; there was no way the DMV could even respond to a message from us about Benjy's awards in the three days necessary for him to get his license in time for the Grand Prix.

"The DMV is just discriminating against people with Asperger's," he fumed. "I should never have even tried. I'll never get to race."

One of his best days had turned sour, and, no matter what I said, I couldn't cheer him. As we quietly walked to the house together, I turned and glared at my nemesis, the Corvair, sitting broken and abandoned. "You still remember how to replace the fan belt?" I asked.

"I have an almost photographic memory, Dad! Remember?!" I had apparently insulted him.

"Well, what do you say? Let's put on our work clothes and do it."

"No, I need to study for the math assessment." Katie had reluctantly agreed to permit Benjy an unusual third and absolutely final try at the math assessment after I begged shamelessly, invoking Benjy's "disability"—precisely the kind of special treatment he loathed.

"What do you say we celebrate your big day by fixing this car? What about having this Corvair ready for you to drive when that letter comes from the DMV?"

"I'm going to college, Dad! I need to learn math."

"You don't have to go to college tonight. You have other nights to study." I could barely believe I had to beg him to play hooky for a few measly hours, especially when the alternative was studying for that detestable test. "As your father, I am allowing you to take a night off. I won't tell anyone."

He considered this highly unusual act of irresponsibility. Fixing the Corvair wasn't on today's schedule for him. It verged on anarchy. But he finally agreed, saying, "Okay! I hate that test!"

We donned work clothes, then met at the Corvair. I rolled up my sleeves, opened the engine compartment, took a deep breath, and then tried to summon my flagging courage. Gone were all thoughts of the satisfaction and accomplishment and fulfillment and pride and Zen that came from working with my own two hands to fix this car. Instead, with my own two hands quivering, I just wanted it over and done with. For I had not ignored or forgotten this repair job over the past weeks; rather, I had obsessed over it. On this routine repair that took most halfway competent Weekend Wrench Warriors no more than 15 minutes, I had compulsively prepared as if I were performing my first brain surgery. Wally, the car's former owner, had sent me his own directions and encouragement. Various Corvair websites contained detailed instructions I had downloaded. Corvair repair manuals and how-to books served up intricate, busy diagrams. YouTube videos purported to show how easy the operation was, one taunting that it was "so easy a caveman could do it with one hand tied behind his back, if his five year-old hadn't fixed it first." All this should have given me confidence. Instead, Kenny's cackle filled my brain; I was sure to hear it after I inevitably failed.

I did consider hiring a professional. I even thought about calling Kenny to come help. In fact, I was thinking hard about it right now as I stared at the beltless engine. But I had watched and read, and watched and read again. I was prepared. And I had my son here to assist; he knew how to do replace this belt better than I did. We would experience quality time now working together on the car. The heck with Kenny's cackle; let it ring in my ears all night. I would not back down from this challenge now. No! I could do this!

"Dad," Benjy prodded, interrupting my reverie.

"What?"

"You're just standing there like you're stuck."

"Yeah, so I am."

"When I get stuck on something, you tell me to get un-stuck."

"That's good advice. I will now get un-stuck."

"We should start. It'll get dark."

"I'm just making sure all my ducks are in a row."

"What ducks?"

"It's just an expression. It means to be fully prepared."

"We should call Kenny. He says he can do it in five minutes with his eyes closed."

"We are not calling Kenny. I can do this. If you have the guts to face that math test again, I sure as hell should have the guts to face this, don't you think?"

Benjy drew a blank. "I don't see the connection," he said, then added, "Dad, the mosquitoes will be out soon. I don't like mosquitoes biting me."

I firmly urged myself on, telling myself out loud, "I have the right tools. I have the right part. I have the knowledge. I have the skill. I have the tenacity. I have fully prepared myself to confront and conquer this challenge. I am ready."

"Dad, you're talking to yourself. You always tell me not to talk to myself."

"That's good advice. I'm just trying to psych myself up." Still paralyzed, I stared at the engine.

"We should call Kenny," Benjy repeated.

I was not calling Kenny. In fact, Benjy's repetitive suggestion unstuck me. It was the push I needed. "So which set of instructions do you remember?"

"All of them."

"I liked Wally's best. They were conversational. No jargon. Let's try those."

"Okay," he said. He started flapping his hand and pacing; it helped him recall the instructions, as if they were orchestral music and he was the conductor waving an imaginary baton. "First, remove the air cleaner housing above the turkey roaster."

"Turkey roaster?" I questioned. I removed the air cleaner housing and stared at the engine. What the heck was the turkey roaster?

Benjy stopped pacing and joined me in staring at the engine. "Dad, if a Corvair can roast turkeys, can it also roast the ducks in the row?"

I laughed at his joke, then realized it was not a joke. I eyed the black arched engine shroud that covered the engine's innards. "I'll bet this big shroud is the turkey roaster," I told him. "It sort of looks like the big black enamel thing we roast the Thanksgiving turkey in."

"We don't roast a turkey," Benjy corrected. "We buy a cooked one from the grocery store." It was true; we hadn't cooked a turkey since Annie died.

"Okay, let's keep moving. That's the turkey roaster. I'm sure of it. What's the next instruction?"

"Dad," he said, not satisfied. "Calling that a turkey roaster if it doesn't really roast turkeys is jargon. You said 'no jargon.'"

"That's good advice. But I'm making an exception for good jargon that metaphorically speaks to me and will help me fix this. Let's keep moving. What's Wally's next instruction?"

Benjy eyed me, hung up on the idea of jargon that spoke metaphorically.

"Next instruction," I prodded. "Keep moving."

Benjy didn't move and kept his big brown eyes trained on me. "You tell me to communicate clearly when I ask you my questions," he went on, growing perturbed. "This time, you didn't communicate clearly with me. You said 'no jargon,' but then you said that some jargon is okay. How am I supposed to know which jargon is good jargon?"

"When you're working with Kenny, do you have these discussions?" I was growing perturbed myself. "Don't you keep moving?"

"Kenny communicates clearly. Unlike some people I won't name."

"I see. Well, we're off to a flying stop here." The sun was sinking. "Can you give me the next instruction, please?"

He eyed me again, processing my words. Flying stop? What? He drew a blank.

"That was a joke, Benjy. The expression is usually 'we're off to a flying start,' and we're not, so I made this dumb little joke—that we're off to a flying stop."

"It's not all my fault that I don't understand your jokes," Benjy complained. "If you told better jokes, maybe I would understand them."

"You are right. It's not your fault at all, I do need better jokes. I apologize. And I'm not laughing at you, I'm laughing with you because this is a fifteen-minute job and at the rate we're going, we may not finish in fifteen years. So no more jokes, word play, jargon, failures to communicate, okay? Just tell me the next instruction."

"You keep saying all the things you tell me are good advice, but you don't obey any of them yourself. Why does good advice only apply to me? That's discrimination."

"I promise I will take my own good advice from now on," I sighed. "Please, Benjy," I begged, "what is the next instruction?"

After 20 minutes of work buried within two hours of questions, clarifications, miscommunications, cajoling, confusion, and begging, the sun had dropped down in exhaustion, and Benjy and I were about to do the same. At last I tightened the wing nut that secured the air cleaner housing. It was over. The Corvair had a new fan belt. Whether it would work or not—who knew?

Before I started the car, I ordered Benjy to take cover just in case the Corvair threw the belt. As I sat behind the wheel, I murmured a silent prayer. Then I turned the key. The balky engine finally turned over, the GEN/FAN warning light burned bright orange—and then dimmed. The car idled peacefully.

I returned to the engine, waiting for an explosion, smoke, flames, coughing, wheezing—anything that betrayed failure. But the belt freely made its way above the turkey roaster, over the alternator pulley, turned down 90 degrees to circle the crank below, then rose up again over what I thought was called the idler, making another 90-degree turn to the fan, and then circled around again. Just like the diagram showed.

As the seconds became minutes, and darkness enveloped us, I finally began to feel the satisfaction. The karma. The nirvana. My own two hands, guided by Benjy's instructions, had created order and usefulness out of mechanical dysfunction. I had become a Doctor Frankenstein, giving life to a dead pile of parts.

"We're getting ice cream, dude!" I yelled triumphantly.

"Dad, it's only a fan belt," Benjy said, still taking cover near the front door. He slapped his cheek, then his arm. The mosquitoes had arrived.

I wasn't about to let minor details burst my karmic bubble. "We've got a lot to celebrate! C'mon! Your awards! This fan belt! We're having an amazing day! We're hot! We should buy lottery tickets!"

"That's gambling, Dad. You always say the lottery is a waste of money."

"So let's go waste some money! We need to test the fan belt out on the road anyway."

"The mosquitoes are out. I may have been bitten. They can carry diseases, you know."

"I've got bug spray in the garage," I countered. "I'll get it."

Benjy yawned. "I don't want to be in the car if it breaks down in the dark. I'm going to bed." He retreated into the house.

Finding a flashlight, I shined it on the engine and watched the fan belt slither easily around the engine for minute after mesmerizing minute. Then I shook myself, as I recalled similarly basking in triumphant satisfaction after installing the seat belts and rotating the tires, neither of which turned out to be, in Benjy's phrase, "all that we'd hoped for." He was right; the new fan belt might not survive five minutes out on the highway. Circumspect humility was in order. It was better to test the car during the day, in case I'd screwed it up again.

Besides, without Benjy around to joy ride with me, there was no satisfaction or triumph. The Corvair, I realized, was not the end; it was the means to the end, which was sharing something with Benjy in a way we'd never shared anything else. I turned the engine off and went to bed. We would road test it together tomorrow.

CHAPTER 14

The next day, after returning from school, Benjy stuck his head into my office and asked, "Did the envelope from the DMV come?"

I handed him the envelope. He eyed it for a moment, as if unable to believe that it had actually come. "Aren't ya gonna open it?" I asked.

"The last letter I got wasn't good," he said, referring to his rejection by Wheeler. He eyed the envelope as if his entire future depended on its contents. Finally, his hands trembling, he ripped it open. His eyes ran over the words, digesting each one, as if he was memorizing them. I had my words of consolation ready. As had been the case with Wheeler, a letter that arrived too soon had to be a rejection.

"They said I can take the learner's permit test," he finally announced, without any note of celebration.

"What?" I sputtered, stunned. "Wow. That's great," I finally managed to get out. He handed me the letter to read. "You see, they didn't discriminate against you," I said. "They were very fair. And prompt." For which I cursed them. There were still more than 30 days to the race—enough time for Benjy to turn his learner's permit into a driver's license.

"I have to send them a doctor's report every year," he groused. "You don't have to do that, do you?"

"No, you're right, they are treating you differently. But you take meds that might impact your ability to drive and I don't. It seems fair to me that they monitor that."

Benjy shrugged, un-persuaded. "We should go to the DMV. It's only open another one hour and six minutes."

I agreed. In the driveway, we came to the crossroads between automobiles. Down one path lay the Toyota. Down the other lay the Corvair, which I had allegedly fixed last night. One path led to boring yet reliable. The other led to innovative yet temperamental, and another possible fan-belt break before we reached the DMV. "Better safe than sorry," I said. "Let's take the Toyota."

"Corvair," Benjy shot back.

"What if the fan belt breaks again?" I asked. "We won't get to the DMV before it closes, and you'll lose another day."

"It won't break," Benjy said confidently. "You did it right."

"I thought I did the wheels right," I pointed out.

"You did that yourself," he pointed out right back. "You should have waited for me to help you. We installed the rear seat belts together and they're okay. Except for the rust prevention."

I relented and held my breath as I turned the Corvair key. The starter cranked until the engine sputtered; each of the six cylinders marched to the beat of a different drummer until they all fell in line, a single synchronized aluminum dance team. I let the motor warm, then punched the accelerator hard a few times to stress the fan belt, reasoning that if I was going to break it, I might as well break it now, in our driveway, so we could take the Camry.

"It'll be fine, Dad," Benjy scolded.

He was right, it was fine. Less than an hour later, Benjy had his learner's permit. The Corvair had performed flawlessly and so had he; he hadn't missed a single question on the written driving exam. The road test to get his full driver's license—that might be another story.

"My dad held autocross races here, back in the day," Kenny mused as he looked out to his field. He had mowed it low and had scattered orange safety cones across it, creating a course that weaved around the old rusting Corvairs.

"What's autocross?" Benjy wanted to know. He had insisted we drive straight here from the DMV for his first lesson behind the wheel.

"Racing one car at a time around the cones," explained Kenny. "Tight turns, shallow turns, long straightaways, short sprints—wherever you drop the cones, it's always a different course. Fastest time wins." He eyed Benjy seriously. "But don't get any ideas about a fast time, Kid, at least not yet. You ain't even driven a car. You go slow and steady."

"I know, I know," said Benjy impatiently.

"Besides," said Kenny, "a good driver always makes sure his vehicle is ready to drive. Right? That it's not going to break down."

"Right!" agreed Benjy.

"So let's check that new fan belt," Kenny grinned, winking at me, which he thought would get my goat. But, in fact, I wanted him to check my handiwork. I was sick of calling the wrecker. And I was gaining confidence; the Corvair's engine had whined at just the same pitch as before on the long drive to Kenny's. No squeaks or squeals signaled that I had fouled up.

Still, I braced myself for Kenny's inevitable onslaught of Dad the Doofus jokes and the news that I had blown yet another repair. With trepidation, I lifted the Corvair's engine cover for his inspection. "It's still on there," he observed, "which is a good sign." He reached in and squeezed the belt. "Lotta slack," he harrumphed, disapprovingly.

"It's supposed to be slack," I bravely shot back. "Right, Benjy?"

"Do not over-tighten the belt," Benjy recited from memory. "Tension is correct when you can rotate the alternator pulley with one finger, but not spin it."

"I was testing you," confessed Kenny. "Feels just right." But then he suddenly got very serious. "Uh oh. What's this? What in the heck have you done to this engine? Benjy, please get me a 9/16th inch socket and ratchet handle."

"What?" I demanded, peering into the engine over Kenny's shoulder. Had I managed yet again to butcher a repair?

"This belt guide is dangling," laughed Kenny, fingering the guide to show me. "You gotta get it up, Man!" He lifted it, then let it drop, again and again, cackling. "You cain't keep it up!"

I cursed myself. How could I have missed it?

"No biggie," said Kenny, as Benjy returned with the correct tools.

"Look at my apprentice here, I couldn't do a thing without him," he complimented. With a few quick moves, he twisted a bolt with the socket wrench, lifted the guide, then snugged the bolt tight again.

"Thanks," I said. "Glad you caught that."

"They didn't even install this guide on the Early Models," Kenny said, "so it really isn't a big deal. But if you're gonna do something, might as well do it right. Right, Kid?"

"Right," agreed Benjy.

"Still," Kenny conceded, "you didn't over-tighten the belt like most people do so that it breaks again in a month. For a couple of first timers who don't know a fan belt from a French fry, it's not half bad."

Benjy raised his hand. "High five, Dad."

I gave Benjy's hand a powerful slap. Psychic and karmic satisfaction coursed through my veins.

"Can I drive now?" he then asked.

"No," I said. "The DMV gave us this nice guide about learning how to drive. And the first lesson is to get to know the car, outside and in."

"I already know the Corvair, outside and in," Benjy insisted. "Can't I drive it now?"

"No," I said again, firmly.

Benjy looked over to Kenny before he decided whether to protest. "Lesson One is Lesson One," Kenny shrugged. "Might as well do it right."

Benjy rarely relented, but Kenny persuaded him. "I will start with Lesson One," he announced.

Three decades earlier, in a remote parking lot at the Pentagon, where my father worked as a civilian accountant, I sat for the first time behind the wheel of his blue four-door Corvair. It was a Saturday, Dad's day off and the day after I'd received my own learner's permit. The usually packed lots were empty, crisscrossed by a parking grid of horizontal and vertical white lines. It was the perfect place, thought Dad, for him to teach me how to drive.

Now I tried to impart Dad's lessons to his grandson. I taught him the eccentricities of GM's Powerglide transmission, a primitive two-forward speed contraption controlled by a lever extruding from the dash-board. Powerglide had settings for Reverse, Neutral, Drive, and Low, but no Park. "To park the car, you use the foot brake to come to a complete stop, then pull up hard on the parking brake, then put the transmission in Neutral, then turn the key to off," I instructed Benjy. "Otherwise, the car might roll."

"I know, Dad, you've told me." In fact, in the weeks we waited for his medical review, Benjy had relentlessly interrogated me on every possible detail of how to drive our Corvair, soaking everything up with his relentless focus. But, now that he was behind the wheel, I told him everything all over again. I instructed him to pull the manual parking brake lever up to see if he had the strength to lift it all the way to the full position. He grunted, then used two hands, and succeeded. With no power assist, I thought turning the steering wheel might be a challenge when the car was stopped. It wasn't; he swung it around easily, despite his theatrical grunts, each followed by "I'm okay!" Then, with a big "duh" in his tone, he reminded me, "There's almost no weight over a Corvair's front wheels, Dad. That's why power steering was never offered on a Corvair, even as an option."

I taught him the quirky old-school controls of the car: the balky levers for the fan, heat, and defrost; the foot switch for the high-beam headlights; the cryptic GM shorthand on the warning lights—TEMP for overheating engine, PRESS for zero oil pressure, GEN for loss of electric generation, and FAN for the failure of the fan that distributes life-giving air to the air-cooled engine, the light that blazed after our fan belt broke.

"You gonna park in my field all day and yak, or are you gonna drive?" Kenny shouted, clutching a beer.

Benjy never heard the taunt; he was concentrating too hard on making lists in his mind to guide him, murmuring them to himself over and over, trying to overcome with preparation and knowledge the challenges that Asperger's had handed him. He struggled to focus on his driving; he knew he couldn't silence the random off-topic thoughts racing through his head, but perhaps, with practice and concentration, he would tune them out.

"Okay, I'm ready," he said finally. Yet again, we went over the long preflight checklist we'd prepared together. He put his fingers on the Corvair's tiny key and looked to me; I nodded back that he was cleared for takeoff. He turned the key and the starter engaged—a sharp, whiny throat-clearing screech. Benjy flinched and let go of the key. "Whoopsie," he said, embarrassed.

"When I learned on one of these with my father, I did the same thing," I said. I hoped it was true. I couldn't remember.

He went over his list again, then turned the key and cranked the starter until the engine caught. After a hiccup or two, the six cylinders purred for him. He cautiously pulled the transmission handle down to Drive, then with all his might yanked up the parking brake to release it. Cautiously, he lightened up his foot pressure on the brake pedal, and the Corvair inched forward, just as another '65 Corvair had in a Pentagon parking lot three decades earlier.

"You're driving," I said. "Congratulations."

He ignored me, focused fully on the path ahead. His lips moved, but I couldn't hear. Riding the brake, he eased the Corvair around the first orange cone, then steered it toward the second.

"Is it the best car you've ever driven?" I joked.

"Be quiet, Dad!"

"Hey, Dale Earnhardt!" razzed Kenny. "Throttle back! Ease off!"

I dropped my arm below the window where Benjy couldn't see it and waved Kenny off from any more razzing. He didn't say another word for the next hour.

And neither did I, as Benjy gently maneuvered among the safety cones, never coming close to testing the Powerglide's second gear.

"He'll get there," I could hear Annie saying as we crept along, just as she'd said so many times over the years, usually after I'd grown impatient with Benjy's deliberateness. "But it'll be in his own way and at his own speed."

I turned back to check the rear seat. And she was there, right beside my father, wearing the new seats belts we'd installed, along for the ride and beaming proudly as Benjy tiptoed the Corvair across Kenny's field. Of course, I was proud, too. But I was also worried; thanks to the

DMV's amazingly unexpected efficiency, in a month Benjy could be racing. I turned back to Annie and Dad to see what they thought about that, and they had vanished.

CHAPTER 15

Befitting his prior service in the Marines, Brad Tripanek stood at attention as I opened our front door to him. Starched shirt and tie, crisply pressed khakis, a clipboard in one hand, he exuded no-nonsense professionalism. He extended his hand to me and delivered a bone-crusher of a shake. "We can teach anyone to drive," he proudly stated after introductions. Of course, I already knew that; his company's slogan was plastered all over its website, as well as the side of his car. That's why I called him.

I could have taught Benjy to drive. I'd already spent dozens of hours teaching Benjy, using the DMV's training guide for parents. But Benjy was unique, of course, and I wanted him to have top-quality professional instruction.

I didn't tell Brad much in advance about Benjy. After all, if he could teach anyone how to drive, how much did he really need to know? But now that he was here, I realized I should have mentioned a few things. Like not to shake Benjy's hand too hard.

"OWWWWWW!" wailed Benjy after Brad delivered his bone-crusher. "You hurt my hand! Why did you do that? My hand is hurt now! I may not be able to grip the steering wheel! I could have several broken bones!"

"The Marine Death Grip," kidded Brad, as he sized Benjy up with the "I Don't Quite Know What's Different, But There is Definitely Something Different About You" look.

I explained about Benjy's Asperger's. Brad hadn't heard of it. As

Benjy tested his injured right hand by flapping it a few times, Brad apologized, "I'm sorry, I didn't mean to hurt you."

"I always do this," Benjy explained about his hand-flapping. "If I couldn't do it, I would be very tense. You should be more careful."

"I certainly will," promised Brad.

"The DMV reviewed Benjy's medical condition and has approved him to drive," I told Brad. "If he passes the standard road test, of course." I showed him the DMV letter, and we discussed Benjy's focus and reaction time.

"Outstanding briefing," said Brad. "I understand the tactical situation and the mission, so let's get started. Benjy, my plan is to drive you over to our office. We have a simulator there. State-of-the-art. We'll acclimate you to the feel of driving a car, discuss defensive driving theory, prepare for conditions you'll face in live-action driving, that sort of thing. How does that sound? Does that sound like a good plan that will accomplish our mission of having you get your driver's license?"

Benjy agreed it sounded like a good plan.

"Let me show you our training vehicle." Brad opened the driver's door to his car. "First, we'll drive it around our closed course, then eventually graduate to the open road. I'll be in the passenger seat, offering guidance as appropriate. If necessary, I can easily assume control of the vehicle. So while it's completely natural and common for new drivers to be anxious when they first get behind the wheel, there's nothing to worry about. We are a team, and together we will accomplish our mission of having you get your driver's license."

"We should take the Corvair," said Benjy. "It doesn't have a driveshaft hump in the floor like that car. It has a rear engine and rear-wheel drive, so there is no need for a driveshaft. So the Corvair is a better car to learn to drive in, because you won't need to reach over a hump to assist me. By the time you do that in your car, I may have caused an accident."

"Yes, that is a beautiful antique," Brad smiled patiently. "But this is our training vehicle. We do all our training in this vehicle. I cannot train you in your vehicle."

"Has that car ever been recalled by its manufacturer?" Benjy asked.

"I believe we did take it in," Brad confessed. "For a non-safety issue. Which has been fixed."

Benjy adamantly shook his head. "I want to learn in the Corvair. It's a better car to learn in."

I gently explained that Brad wasn't saying the Corvair was inferior to his car, that he hadn't intended to slight the Corvair. Brad was accustomed to training using his vehicle. His company required him to use his vehicle. He simply had to use his vehicle or else he couldn't teach Benjy.

Benjy considered it. I thought I'd persuaded him. Then he shook his head. Fundamental principles were at stake. "No, thank you," he said politely. "The Corvair is a better car to accomplish our mission of having me get my driver's license. Since I'll be driving the Corvair, I should learn to drive the Corvair."

"Lord knows I'm no fan of Ralph Nader," said Brad, trying hard to connect with Benjy, and nicely ignoring Benjy's echoing of his language, which some would've taken as mocking. "This was the car he said was unsafe at any speed. Right?"

The mention of Nader caused Benjy to explain in excruciating detail the difference between the engineering of the Early Model Corvair—wrongly implicated by Nader, he said—and our Late Model, with its highly praised, state-of-the-art four-wheel independent suspension based on a design GM had engineered for the top-of-the-line Corvette.

"Look," said Brad, raising his hands in surrender, his patience nearly exhausted. "The problem, Benjy, is our insurance. We're only covered for injuries and accidents with clients when we use our training vehicle. Because the insurance company knows our vehicle. They don't know yours. That's not to disparage your Corvair. My aunt had a Corvair she was very fond of. But I can't teach you in a vehicle I'm not insured in. You wouldn't want that either, you'd want me to be insured in case something happened. That makes sense, doesn't it?"

"No," said Benjy.

"Why not?" asked Brad.

"Because," started Benjy, who then, like a slow but steady volcanic eruption, unstoppably spewed hot facts and scalding opinions throughout a speech that began with the fallacies behind Nader's conclusions, then broadened to include discrimination against people with differences, and climaxed with the unfairness of insurance companies that didn't appreciate the marvels of the unjustly stigmatized Corvair, the most innovative and best-engineered car in the history of the universe, and the ideal car in which to learn how to drive.

At this stem-winder's four-minute mark, all traces of a smile had vanished from Brad's face. At eight minutes, he checked his watch and looked over to me, pleading for an interruption. Then he cleared his throat. Loudly. Like a locomotive.

But Benjy did not catch this obvious social cue that practically screamed, "Hey, kid, enough already." I decided not to intervene; it was obvious that Benjy wouldn't let Brad teach him how to drive, so why not let him vent? Finally, at the 11-minute mark, as Benjy paused to take a breath, Brad got a word in. "I can't say I followed all of that, but I certainly appreciate how strongly you hold your opinions. Still, the bottom line here is simple. If I can't teach you in my vehicle, then I can't teach you. Period. Over and out."

"The side of your car says 'We can teach anyone,'" Benjy noted. "That's not true. You're not teaching me."

Brad fixed his glare on Benjy. "We can teach anyone," he said tersely, "in our car."

Benjy fixed his eyes on Brad. "Then it should say, 'We can teach anyone to drive if they agree to learn to drive in this car.' Otherwise, it's not true. My dad says I can be too rigid, but I think it is you who are being too rigid. People are different, so there is not always just one right way to teach something. There should be different teaching strategies for different people."

Like others had over the years when Benjy flouted the social niceties and said exactly what he thought, Brad now glared at me as if to ask why wasn't I stepping in to discipline my son? While my son spouted his extreme, rigid, impolite, asocial, insulting opinions, was I just going to stand there like a bump on a log? What kind of ineffective, impolite, pathetic, passive parent was I, anyway? Don't I know that bad parenting causes this kind of inappropriate behavior? And that firm discipline—even a good spanking—would eliminate it?

Over the years, I had in fact apologized many times for Benjy's socially inappropriate behavior. But I had never agreed that his behavior was caused by bad parenting or lack of discipline. Annie was the best parent any child could possibly have, especially a boy like Benjy. And whenever I was at my most exasperated with Benjy's behavior, and wondered if maybe firmer discipline would improve it, she would always caution me to take a deep breath and be patient, that I would not change Benjy, he would change me. It was just Asperger's, and Asperger's could not be disciplined out of him. And she was right.

"He's made several valid points," I said finally. "I'm sorry if we wasted your time."

Exasperated, Brad delivered an even more bone-crushing handshake that left my fingers dangling like overcooked linguine. Then he extended his hand to Benjy. "Good luck to you, young man," he said.

Benjy avoided the handshake; instead, he raised his hand and waved. "Bye," he said. Brad again looked to me as if I had failed as a parent. My throbbing, crumpled hand wished I'd been as socially unconventional as my son.

With school now over, Benjy made what was for him a momentous decision; he changed his daily schedule. The NASCAR video game was out. Now, starting at sun up, he attacked his math assessment tutorials. Hours later, when he could stand no more math, and I could stand no more work, we drove together to Kenny's field and practiced the DMV manual's driving lessons, putt-putting slowly to avoid stirring up dust. Then, as the sun went down, I drove us home, and we both collapsed in bed.

Near dinnertime one afternoon, as Kenny finished guzzling a beer, he asked me skeptically, "Is he gonna be able to take that act on the road?" It was the 10th straight day that Benjy, driving alone, had spent four hours or longer bobbing and weaving our Corvair through the course of orange cones set around its fellow Vairs in the field. "I mean, I don't really care if he drives the race, that's just for laughs. He needs to be safe on the road. You think he will be?"

It was the first time Kenny had spoken seriously to me. I'd had the same thoughts, of course. According to the DMV training manual, we should have left the safe haven of an empty parking lot for the challenge of the open road days ago. I thought Benjy was ready. He had good command of the car. But he declined. He wanted to take things at his own pace, and his pace was cautious. He preferred driving alone in the field, around and around, back and forth. And the Grand Prix was less than three weeks away.

"He ever talk about the race?" Kenny asked.

"Not once since he started driving," I reported. He'd been so obsessed by the race prior to getting his learner's permit that I found it strange.

"That's good!" Kenny exclaimed. "Maybe he's deciding he's not ready yet. Puttin' aside somethin' he had his heart set on. For a teenager, that shows responsibility and maturity." Then he cackled, "Maybe he can teach me some." Hoisting up another beer from his cooler, he plucked the pull tab, considered it, and left the can unopened. "Heck, maybe he already has," he said, and replaced the can in the cooler.

"Can I drive to McDonald's for lunch?" Benjy asked the next day. "With the top down?" I'd have dropped the top even if he hadn't asked; it was a spring day that had sneaked into summer—a brilliant, comfortable sun and no shirt-staining humidity. The convertible's ancient motor reluctantly screeched and whined, even after I greased its gears, but the top eventually came to rest peacefully in its cubby behind the back seat. "Can we put the cover over it now?" Benjy asked. This was a major pain that we'd never done before; we had to stretch the crinkly vinyl boot over the retracted convertible top, then press down with our thumbs over 20 balky metal snaps. But when we were done, our art deco Corvair looked ready to lead a parade.

"What's the occasion?" I probed, wondering if it had something to do with Lydia.

"It just looks better this way," he said.

"And you're ready to drive on the highway?"

"Yes," he said.

"Will we go through the drive-thru window?"

"Yes," he said. "I need the experience of driving through the drive-thru window. It's very narrow and I will be driving through the McDonald's drive-thru a lot."

"I see," I nodded. Yup—Lydia.

I offered to back the Corvair out of our narrow driveway into the street, but Benjy wanted to do it himself. His lips moved as he went through his checklist. When he was ready, he turned the key and held it, and the car started eagerly. Again he whispered to himself as he placed his foot on the brake and lifted the transmission lever from N to R, causing a *thunk*. Then he grunted as he yanked on the parking brake with both hands to release it.

He tentatively eased the car back to the street, looking both ways, stopping, backing up a foot and then a yard at a time until he rolled across the sidewalk and dipped the back wheels over the driveway apron. Halfway into the street now, he stopped and looked both ways, and then looked both ways again. Whispering more instructions to himself, he carefully lifted his foot from the brake pedal so that the car crept back again as he turned the wheel.

For the first time, he was driving on the public street. "Excellent," I said.

He didn't hear me; he was silently murmuring through his next list—the Going From Reverse to Forward List. We sat for a minute on the street like a plane waiting for a gate at the terminal. Then he shifted the transmission lever down two stops to D. We inched forward.

"You are driving on the public street, dude," I crowed. "Congratulations."

"Don't distract me," he scolded. He lifted his foot entirely off the brake and coasted the car to a full stop at the end of our block.

"You're doing better than I did at your age," I applauded. "I never got a Corvair out of the parking lot."

He never heard me, he was concentrating so hard. And now, the Driving Gods smiled on him; like the Red Sea for Moses, the heavy traffic on the main highway parted, allowing him to make an unhurried right turn. Mastering that challenge, he took a breath, whispered a few things to himself, stayed in the right lane, checked his mirrors regularly, and accelerated to half the speed limit as the world whooshed past us in the left lane. After a mile, he took a breath. He was relaxing, gaining confidence. He accelerated slightly.

And then he was screaming. "GET IT AWAY! GET IT AWAY!" he shrieked, stomping on the brake pedal with both feet, screeching the Corvair to a skidding stop and covering his face with his hands.

"What? What's the matter?" I asked, trying to sound calm, but probably shouting, as I turned around and waved my arms frantically to signal the traffic behind us to go around. Thank God the top was down so they could see me.

"THERE'S A LIZARD! GET IT AWAY!"

"I don't see a liz—"

"ON THE FLOOR! GET IT AWAY!"

"Benjy, you've got to move the car to the curb," I said, hoping I still sounded calm. "We could get in a very bad accident here." With a break in the traffic behind us, I wheeled around in my seat, and scanned the interior of the car, trying to spot the serpent.

"I CAN'T!" he wailed. "THERE'S A LIZARD ABOUT TO CRAWL ON ME!"

Even with no driveshaft hump on the Corvair's floor, I could see no lizard.

"Pull the car over to the curb, Benjy," I ordered. "We'll deal with the lizard there."

"I can't," he whimpered. "It's down there."

Suddenly, a pickup truck was behind us, closing too fast. It honked, then swerved to avoid us. "GET THAT PIECE OF SHIT OFF THE ROAD!" the speeding teenager yelled through the open passenger window, giving us a one-finger salute. "WHAT ARE YOU? RETARDED?"

"Take your feet off the brake," I ordered Benjy, "and let the car coast. I'll steer to the curb."

But it was no use. Benjy was frozen. Then I saw it—a black blur with a blue stripe scurried under the brake pedal. It was possibly five inches long.

"Benjy, it's just a skink. Like we have in our garden. It won't hurt you. It's scared of you!"

"I hate lizards! They're not supposed to be in the car!" he said, trembling.

"Benjy, if you want to drive a car—if you want to live independently—I can't always be there for you. You need to do this. You need to pull this car over before we get creamed!"

Finally, Benjy opened his eyes. The skink had disappeared, for the moment at least. He relaxed his taut legs just enough to ease the pressure on the brake pedal. Still trembling, he signaled a right turn, and I steered us to the curb. Then, rushing like it was a NASCAR pit stop, he yanked up the parking brake, put the Corvair in N, turned the engine off, hopped out of the car, slammed the door shut so the skink wouldn't follow him, and raced around the front of the car to the safety of the sidewalk.

"You okay?" I asked, joining him.

"NO!"

He let me put my arm around him. "In all the years I've been driving," I told him softly, "I have never before seen a lizard in a car. Why it happened today, your first time on the road, I have no idea. I'm sorry. The odds are it will not ever happen again. But if it does, you have to react safely. Okay?"

"Okay," he said, putting on his brave face. "I'm fine. I'm okay." But he wasn't okay, he was upset. I put my arm around him, and he didn't pull away. "I'm not retarded," he finally said. "And this car is not what he said it is."

"Forget that guy. He's just another bully. Forget him."

"He was speeding. He was mean! He's the one who shouldn't have a driver's license, not me!"

I squeezed Benjy's shoulders to pull him closer. "There are lots of bad people in the world, and lots of bad drivers on the road," I told him. "That's part of life, unfortunately. Calm down. Don't let it upset you."

"Why can't people be nice?"

"I don't know."

I left Benjy to go on a skink hunt, crawling on the Corvair's carpet to peer behind the dash. I removed the rear seat, pulled up the carpet. Nothing.

"I can't find it. Maybe it's gone," I said.

"We didn't see it crawl out, so it must still be in there," he said.

It turned out our car was partially blocking a driveway. Now a blocked driver wanted to back out, and we needed to move. "Do you want me to drive the car or can you?" I asked, signaling the other driver that we needed a moment.

"Dad, there is a lizard in that car! We can't drive it! It could bite us. We should have it towed."

There was no way I was calling that tow truck driver again.

"It's a skink, Benjy. It's harmless."

"How do you know skinks are harmless? You are not an expert on skinks."

"They aren't harmful, and they don't bite."

"How do you know?!" he demanded. "How do you know it won't bite?"

The driver in the driveway irritably raised his hands—an unmistakable social cue. "Look, Benjy," I pleaded, "I'll drive us to McDonald's from here. But we've got to go. If it was dangerous, I wouldn't get in that car, and I wouldn't ask you to either. So are you going to get in or are you going to walk?"

He didn't move. "You should call the tow truck," he said.

"I will not call the tow truck!" I insisted. "I'm sick of tow trucks. Even if there's a man-eating crocodile in there, I am not calling that tow truck."

Benjy considered his options. "I want to go home," he said. He opened the passenger door, stepped on the seat bottom, slowly maneuvered his rear end onto the seat, brought his knees up to his chest, and wrapped his arms around his legs. As I drove him home, his feet never touched the floor.

CHAPTER 16

"Some skinks are carnivores," Benjy triumphantly reported to me after we returned home; he had marched straight to his computer from the Corvair, determined to get the skinny on skinks. "Carnivores eat meat. Humans are meat. Which means skinks could not only bite humans, but eat humans."

"There are over eight hundred varieties of skinks," I countered, having also marched straight to my own computer to become skink-savvy. "The ones you're talking about are giant skinks from other continents. Here we have garden skinks. Tiny garden skinks. Without teeth. A five-inch skink in a car will not bite the driver."

"You are not a scientific expert," Benjy said in his usual flat tone. "You said Mom couldn't die from the flu, and she did."

I searched Benjy's face for a sign that he wanted to talk or cry or vent, or somehow react to Annie's death. He'd never really expressed his feelings about his mom's passing and rarely mentioned it. Not that I'd expected him to; he rarely expressed personal emotions. But then, riding in the Corvair with Lydia, he'd volunteered that his mother had died. And now he'd raised it with me. Maybe something was happening here—a readiness to express his emotions, perhaps?

"Yes, I did say that," I finally said, "because that's what the doctors told me. It wasn't fair that she died when the odds were so low, was it?"

"No," he agreed. "Just as it wouldn't be fair if a skink bit me while I was driving a Corvair. But it nearly happened. Just because the odds are low doesn't mean it won't happen. You should learn that." He walked away, looking vindicated.

"Hey," I called after him. He stopped at the stairs.

"You just walked away there, while we were still talking, I thought. Talking about Mom. Do you want to say or ask anything, maybe?" I gently prodded.

"We were talking about being bitten by a skink, Dad," he corrected, sounding annoyed. "You always tell me that, in a conversation, I should not change the subject to what I want to talk about, but that's what you just did. You should learn that, too." He bounded up the stairs, two at a time, looking even more vindicated.

"May I drive to McDonald's for lunch?" Benjy asked the next day after he finished his math work. As if the carnivorous skink scare had never happened.

"Are you sure?" I pressed. "When you drive, people are counting on you. You can't panic or get upset or distracted, whether it's by a skink or NASCAR games or *National Treasure*."

"I know," he nodded. "I won't."

"So you've made peace with the possibility of a skink in the car?"

"I want to drive," he shrugged. "Even though it is possible that they bite, at least a skink is not a snake or a crocodile."

Outside, under Benjy's watchful eye, I gave the Corvair another skink inspection. "My bet is it's gone," I said. We had left the Vair's top down and windows open overnight to give the unwelcome intruder plenty of escape routes. "I dunno. Maybe there's some kind of skink repellent we can use?"

"There are no proven skink repellents," Benjy said. "I read that yesterday."

"Maybe we can tune to a radio station that plays music skinks don't like?"

"Dad, you're being silly," he said. This was no laughing matter to him, and I apologized. He stepped into the car as if the floor were on fire. Taking a big gulp of air, then letting it out like a slowly leaking tire, Benjy buckled his seat belt, whispered the preflight checklist to himself, and turned the key. Backing out of the driveway, he kept sneaking peeks down to the floor, searching for our serpent friend. I ordered him to keep his eyes on the road while I became the Skink Scout. "Okay," he said. He added "I am not afraid of skinks" to his murmured checklist.

At the main road, he waited patiently for an opening in traffic while occasionally glancing at the floor. His face was beet red; his pulse must have been off the charts. "Breathe," I insisted. "It's gone." As the traffic cleared, he slowly turned into the right lane.

After barely a block, a speeding driver was on our bumper. As Benjy anxiously checked the mirrors, I quietly advised, "Keep breathing. It's okay. You're doing everything right." The driver pulled up beside us, down came the passenger window, and Benjy lurched toward me, as if bracing to be hit by something thrown from the other car. The speeding driver was no teen; he was closer to my age. Couldn't he show some patience? Hadn't he once driven a car for the first time?

The speeding driver tapped his horn to get our attention, then shouted "Great car!" Benjy refused to look over, instead focusing like a laser on the road ahead. I waved to the driver and gave him a thumbs-up. "My mother had one," the driver yelled as he drove parallel to us. "First car I ever drove!" I gave him another thumbs-up and pointed to Benjy, trying to gesture that it was his first time. The driver returned my thumbs-up, then accelerated ahead of us.

"Stuff happens when you drive such a cool ride," I murmured, smiling, trying to ease Benjy's anxiety.

"Be quiet, Dad," he replied, straightening up in his seat, taut as a piano wire, his gaze never veering from the road ahead. Finally, three cautious miles later, the Golden Arches came into view. He took a deep breath and relaxed.

At the drive-thru, Benjy deftly maneuvered into the lunchtime rush lineup and edged forward until we reached the ordering microphone. "Welcome to McDonald's! May I take your order, please?" a boy's voice squawked from the box. Disappointment descended over Benjy's face—he'd hoped Lydia was working today. He unenthusiastically ordered his Chicken McNuggets, then unhappily inched the Corvair forward to the pick-up window.

"Benjy!" Lydia was at the window, her smile blinding. "You're driving!" She pushed away the purple lock that dangled across her face.

"Yes," said Benjy, suddenly animated. "Why weren't you taking the orders?"

Lydia handed our drinks over to Benjy. "We split that up when it's so busy," she said, then anxiously turned to see if the manager had her under surveillance for Fraternizing With the Customers.

But Benjy didn't pick up on her anxiety; words rushed out of him. "I only have my learner's permit, but, if I pass the road test, then I'll have my driver's license. Then I won't need to have him in the car." He pointed at me. "Like I'm a kid. I'm not a kid anymore. Then I'm going to drive a Corvair in a race called the Grand Prix du Garbage. It's in West Virginia. I made a friend named Kenny. He likes Corvairs, too. He fixed the wheels on this car so they won't fall off ever again. So it's safe to go for a ride."

As Lydia passed Benjy his McNuggets, she replied sweetly, "Benjy, I really, really would like to talk to you, but I can't now."

"There was a skink in the car," Benjy continued as if he hadn't heard her, "but I think it's gone now. And it was probably not carnivorous, although there's no way to tell for sure unless we capture it. I've decided not to be afraid of it, and so should you, if you decide to go for a ride."

"Benjy, I cannot talk now!" Lydia exclaimed. "You'll get me fired!" She slammed her window shut and gestured urgently to Benjy to move on.

Benjy's chin dropped to his chest. "We have to go, Benjy," I told him. "She's working."

Suddenly, a familiar pickup truck screeched to a halt beside us. The driver stuck his head out the window to shout at Lydia, "Hey, Babe, what the hell's the holdup? The line's back to the street!" Benjy and I both recognized him as the bully who jeered at us the day before.

Lydia opened her window, shot another glance back to her manager, then gestured urgently to the pickup driver to go. "Go, Bobby! You'll get me fired!"

"Before you go," I told Bobby, "I think you owe my son an apology for the things you said yesterday when you passed us."

"I didn't say nothin' to you," he smirked. "Babe! Speed it up!" he ordered Lydia. "I'm hungry!"

"You were in that very truck and you certainly did say something very rude to us," I insisted.

Lydia saw instantly that Bobby was lying. "What did you say?" she demanded, eyes ablaze.

"Nothin', I told you. I don't know what he's talkin' about."

"You are lying," Lydia cried. "You lie about everything! You apologize!"

Bobby waved his hand dismissively, spun his tires, and screeched off.

"You lied to me for the last time!" Lydia screamed after him. "JERK!"

A few frustrated drivers stuck in line behind us honked their horns.

"Is he your boyfriend?" Benjy asked. We'd only seen the back of his head while he was smooching Lydia at Senior Day.

"Not anymore!" Upset, she turned away from the window, right into the arms of the McDonald's manager who had been drawn by the commotion. She pushed him aside and ran off, crying.

"Is there something I can help with?" the manager finally asked us, looking bewildered.

"May I have some barbeque sauce for my Chicken McNuggets, please?" Benjy asked.

"That's a very nice car," said the frazzled manager as he dumped a lifetime supply of sauce packets in Benjy's lap. "Would you mind moving it, please?"

For Benjy's third and absolutely final try at the math assessment, Katie greeted us at the door to James Monroe, full of encouragement. "The third time's the charm!" she chirped as we headed to the Learning Center together.

"What does that mean?" Benjy asked, puzzled. "Is that on the test? It wasn't on the tutorial." His mood was not good. He resented having to be here.

"No, no," Katie said, realizing her cliché had eluded Benjy. "Just a saying. Which I said because I'm very confident you're going to do well this time. I know you've been working very hard with your father."

"I'm not working with him. He's worse at math than I am," Benjy reported. "He's the one who should have to take math, not me. I passed all the state's standardized tests in high school."

"I know you did, and that's why you're going to do very well today. I can just feel it." She was irrepressible. She looked at me with a big, inviting smile, then brushed her hair away with her left hand. There was no ring on her ring finger, I noticed. It was the first time since Annie died that I'd looked at a woman's hand to see if she might be available.

"Can we just get this over with?" Benjy asked Katie as she opened up his private test-taking room. Then he unleashed a deafening yawn in which his uncovered mouth opened wide enough to swallow a cantaloupe. "I have to practice my parallel parking. The Corvair doesn't have power steering. And I have to turn the steering wheel a lot to park it because it's a slow-ratio steering gearbox. We don't have the quick-ratio steering gearbox. A lot of Corvair owners like that better because it makes the wheels turn faster. I think I'd like it better. Ours takes a lot of muscles." I now realized that Benjy had spent a lot of his scheduled math tutorial time on instead methodically working his way through Google's 9,460,000 search results for the Corvair.

Katie nodded her head as if she knew exactly what Benjy was talking about—I'm glad one of us knew, because I had no clue. "Well, there's your math all coming back!" she chirped. "You know your ratios! See, you really will do just fine!"

"Benjy," I gently chided, "you need to focus on your math test now. You can save yourself a couple of years of math courses you don't want to take, so this is the top priority. Right?"

"Sure, sure, sure," he said, plopping down in front of the computer, as if awaiting his turn to have his head guillotined. "The test created by normals for normals that has nothing to do with me." His calculator, pencils, and scratch paper were beside him. "Could you leave, please?" he ordered me. "You're not allowed in here. You'd only give me the wrong answers anyway."

After Katie closed the door, we each let out a big sigh and laughed at his extreme grumpiness. "Sorry about that," I said, once we were beyond Benjy's hearing. "Sometimes he lets you know exactly what he's thinking, and sometimes you have no idea."

"I think I know which today was," Katie laughed. "He's very smart and very sweet and I know he'll do just fine here. And our remedial math teachers are excellent with students with disabilities."

"I'm pleased to hear that," I said, "because it looks like he'll be spending a lot of time with them." I meant it to be a joke, sort of, and we both smiled. And if I had been someone else, I might then have asked Katie if I could buy her a cup of coffee? But I was not someone else; I was a lot like Benjy, and I was in an equally foul mood. "I still don't understand why Benjy has to even take this test," I vented. "He took math in high school. He passed it. The state certified it. He doesn't want to be a mathematician. He doesn't want to be an engineer or scientist. He wants to come to college to read books. To study history and psychology and political science and public speaking and theater. He takes pleasure in those things. He might be a public speaker in the future—an evangelist for people who are different. He has a talent for it. Isn't that a good thing to encourage? So why must we erect this hurdle for him? On his cell phone, he has a calculator that can do more math than he will ever need. On a computer, he can ask Google any math question and get the right answer back in a fraction of a second. Why must he start college, which should be such a positive, wonderful, rewarding experience for him, by being forced to repeat the torture he endured in high school? I know everyone says America needs to develop mathematicians and scientists and engineers so we can compete with China and India. But isn't there still a place in America for someone who doesn't know math, but loves to read and write and speak and think, and has such a unique view of the world? His eagerness to learn should be nurtured, not snuffed out by having to conform to this arbitrary pre-computer pre-calculator requirement that has absolutely nothing to do with him or his future. Why can't this school accommodate that?"

As my tirade grew increasingly heated, Katie's smile slowly descended into a frown. "We are not torturing students here," she replied testily, once I gave her a chance to speak. "And I am certainly not about snuffing out a student's eagerness to learn, I assure you."

"I know, I'm sorry," I muttered. But I couldn't shut myself up. "It's just that he has enough of the deck stacked against him. I don't see why you have to make it worse."

"Me?!" Katie exclaimed. "I'm bending over backwards to help him. I'm breaking the rules to let him take this test over and over."

"I meant the school, not you personally," I backpedaled. "I'm sorry, it came out wrong."

"This school—and I—we are not about erecting barriers to anyone!" Katie insisted. "Especially students with disabilities. We are about teaching and graduating educated citizens. Certainly college math will be difficult for him. But that's not a reason he should avoid it. That's a reason he should work hard and succeed at it, and he will, with our help. I have every confidence in him. And so should you."

"I do have every confidence in him," I said. "It's the world I'm worried about."

"If you'll excuse me, I have some work to attend to," Katie said, already striding away from me.

That cup of coffee I'd hoped to buy Katie now appeared to be out of the question. How could I be so inappropriate and insulting? To someone who was trying to help my son, not hurt him? Was this my Asperger's rearing its ugly head? Or was that just a way for me to excuse myself for being such a pontificating bore?

Back at home, I brewed a big pot of coffee, sent Katie a hugely apologetic e-mail, and waited for Benjy's phone call to come pick him up. I hoped against hope that the first words out of his mouth were anything other than, "Dad, it wasn't all that we'd hoped for."

Benjy had three hours to complete the test. So when the phone rang after 90 minutes and I saw his cell phone number on the Caller I.D., I knew it was trouble.

"Dad," he said when I answered, his voice betraying his defeat. "It wasn't all that we'd hoped for."

Returning to James Monroe, the Corvair seemed to drive as if the road were paved with glue; as it crawled along, I turned over and over in my mind the best way to react to the bad news. What could I say to stop Benjy from becoming dispirited and angry? I was so dispirited and angry myself that I was drawing a blank. I drove slower, or the glue became stickier, but eventually the Corvair found its way to the school. Outside the front door, Benjy paced, hopping up onto the tips of his Size 13's with each step, flapping his hand and reciting. He was ready to detonate, that was obvious. He came over to the driver's door, expecting to drive. I had to think of something fast.

"Hold on a sec," I said. "Let's talk about what happened. I don't want you to drive while you're upset."

"I'm fine," he said tersely. When I pressed him for details of the test, he bristled. "I didn't do as well as we'd hoped," he repeated. "I still have to take math."

"Okay, but which math?" I pressed. "How much math? Come on, let's talk about this first."

"College math," he replied, annoyed. "A year of college math."

"But what about the two and a half years of remedial math before the college math?"

"Ms. Baxter said I don't have to take it because I got a better score this time. But I still have to take the college math. Which I don't want to take and I think they should not force me to take."

"Do I understand this right?" I said carefully. "Your score today was so good that you don't have to take any remedial math at all?"

"I just said that, Dad," he said, even more annoyed. "You're repeating what I just said."

"But that's wonderful news, Benjy! You just saved yourself from taking two and a half years of remedial math! Aren't you excited?"

He stared at me like I was hopelessly thick. "But I still have to take a whole year of college math. Which I don't want to do!"

"We should be celebrating, not shouting. This is fantastic news. Let's go anywhere you want for lunch. The finest restaurant in town. The finest in the world!" I hopped out and turned the Corvair over to him.

"Dad?" he said, buckling his safety harness.

"Yes?"

"Ms. Baxter said to tell you she told you so."

"Okay, thanks for telling me."

"Did she say that because you thought I was going to fail?"

I sighed. "To be honest, based on your other two tries, yes, I did. Sorry."

"That's okay. I did, too."

He headed to McDonald's, of course, driving confidently, with very little whispering to himself. There were no frenzied skink hunts or fearful discussions. He didn't object when I asked him questions. And I had plenty of questions about this amazing reversal of fortune.

"Was anything different about the test this time?" I asked cautiously, not wanting in any way to disparage his triumph. "I mean, no one came into the private room. Right?"

"That would be cheating, Dad," he said. "I just suddenly saw the answers this time, like I was back in high school and saw it all on the board. I saw all the formulas and definitions, and all the examples. It was all there in my head and I suddenly found it."

"You just made your college life a lot more fun," I said, amazed.

Benjy had other things on his mind as he placed his McNuggets order and pulled up to the drive-thru window, where a teenage boy was working. Benjy shifted in his seat to see if he could glimpse Lydia somewhere in the back, then looked over to me, discouraged.

"Ask where she is," I prodded.

"Is Lydia here?" he finally asked the new window worker.

"She got fired," the boy replied. "You can read all about it on Facebook." He stuck his head out the window and checked on the line behind us. "I have to keep this line moving," he said. "Hint, hint."

Benjy got the hint and handed me the McNuggets. Then he steered the Corvair away from the window to the highway.

"Don't you want to eat in the parking lot?" I asked. "Like we always do?"

"No, thank you," he said.

Once we returned home, he went to his room and climbed under the covers. His grand celebration Chicken McNuggets remained behind on the kitchen counter, untouched.

CHAPTER 17

"You're taking your road test in *that*?" the DMV road test examiner thundered incredulously. "They call it a Deathmobile, you know. For a very good reason." I couldn't tell if it was the summer heat and humidity radiating off the asphalt of the DMV parking lot or the examiner's foul mood that caused heat waves to rise up off his shaved head.

He looked like he could use a funny story, I thought. Like my own Deathmobile story. And then I realized his scowl and glare spoke volumes. I read the social cues. My funny story could wait.

But Benjy didn't recognize those same social cues; he didn't see that we ought to immediately take the Corvair home and return with the Toyota, and then beg the examiner's forgiveness. Instead, he had already launched a lecture on how only misinformed people believed that the Corvair was a Deathmobile.

The examiner's glare intensified, but Benjy's lecture continued, turning to the question of whether the Corvair should be called the World's Greatest Car. Finally, the examiner cut Benjy off, snapping, "Look, all I care about is whether it's properly registered and passed the safety inspection, and if you can drive it safely. And air conditioning would be nice." Perspiration soaked his shirt.

I produced the car's registration and safety inspection certificate while Benjy helpfully noted that "air conditioning was an extra-cost option in many Corvairs, except for the turbocharged model. This is not a turbocharged model, but it does not have the air conditioning option."

The examiner gave Benjy a long look, trying to decide whether he meant to be mocking. Benjy innocently returned the look, betraying nothing. Frustrated, the examiner snatched the Corvair's paperwork from me. With a theatrical grunt of disdain, he appeared to find it satisfactory, shoved it back to me, then turned his attention to Benjy's driver's license application. "Young man, I see you have a medical condition that has been reviewed. But you must understand that, if you pass the road test today, you have a disability that may potentially impact your ability to drive safely. Therefore, you must drive accordingly at all times, and not drive when medications or a physical or mental condition would impair your ability to drive safely. Is that clear?"

I braced for a Benjy lecture about disability and difference and discrimination that would last an eternity.

"Yes sir," Benjy said.

"Well, I've got to say," said the examiner, launching his own lecture on the merits of the Corvair, or lack thereof, "that driving with a disability in this car is asking for trouble. Are you familiar with the book *Unsafe at Any Speed*? By Ralph Nader? The Corvair is what he wrote about. It's literally unsafe at any speed. Growing up, I lost one of my closest friends in a car accident. He was driving a Corvair."

Wally had warned me about genuine Corvair Haters when I bought the car—people who for whatever reason held a grudge against or could not abide the car. Now we'd finally found one.

In the 30 days that Benjy had driven with his learner's permit, I had vigilantly monitored him from the passenger's seat for the nearly 80 hours he drove the Corvair—twice the minimum requirement—on all kinds of roads, day and night, in all traffic and weather conditions, save for snow and ice. Now his final hurdle to receiving his driver's license was to pass the DMV road test. It was also his final hurdle to racing in tomorrow's Grand Prix du Garbage. But state law prohibited a driver's license applicant from taking his or her road test more than once per day. So this was it; Benjy's one and only chance to obtain the license that would allow him to race tomorrow. With a genuine Corvair Hater as his examiner, I calculated the odds on his racing tomorrow at approximately zero.

"Maybe we should go home and return with the Camry?" I asked Benjy.

"NO!" Benjy thundered. "The Corvair is not an unsafe car! It's not true! It's not fair!"

As Benjy prepared to deliver his greatest peroration yet on the goodness of all things Corvair, I put my hand forcefully on his arm and squeezed, trying to stop him.

"OWWW!" he cried. "That hurts."

I ignored him and turned to the examiner. "We're both very sorry about your friend," I said, in a soothing diplomatic tone that I hoped didn't come across as obvious obsequiousness, which it was. "But to be fair, while there may be a genuine difference of opinion as to the safety of Early Model Corvairs, this is a Late Model Corvair, and the Late Model's safety has never been questioned. It has the suspension and safety improvements that Nader demanded. As you can see, ours has modern front seats, headrests, and seat and shoulder belts installed. If I felt there was any question about whether this car was safe, as his father, I wouldn't let him drive it. And I wouldn't drive it either."

I searched the examiner's baking face to see if I'd made any headway. In that momentary silence, Benjy seized the initiative. "On August 12, 1972," he boomed, "the United States Government wrote a letter to every Corvair owner." Perhaps I could have squeezed his arm again to quiet him. Perhaps I could have interrupted him. And I had already tried to help—to be diplomatic and suggest getting the Camry. But he had a statement to make about injustice and fairness and tolerance. He wanted to take a stand. He was a young adult now, striving to live independently, and I wouldn't—couldn't—always be there for him. There would be difficult situations for him to navigate where he'd be on his own, and this might as well be one of them.

Those were my lofty well-intended reasons for me not to intervene. I also had another reason, perhaps less well-intended and more devious. If Benjy didn't get his driver's license today, from this fuming examiner, then he couldn't race tomorrow, and I wouldn't be the Bad Guy. In fact, I realized my earlier efforts at diplomacy and mediation were misguided. Instead, I wanted Benjy to tell him every last detail about the Corvair that Google could produce, and talk until the sun went down. Bring it on, Benjy! Tell him about the Corvair fanatics who search for the first and the last Corvairs ever built (neither has been found)! Tell him anything, just keep telling him! Forgive me, Benjy, and Annie, and Dad, for I have sinned.

Words extolling the Corvair flowed out of Benjy the way water flowed over Niagara Falls: in a ceaseless, monotonous, forceful torrent, with the beginning long forgotten and no end in sight. Judging by the examiner's narrowing eyes, shifting feet, soaking shirt, and throat clearings, Benjy's chance to get his driver's license today had melted away like last winter's ice. Yet Benjy droned on, wrapping up Corvair 101 and immediately launching into the Honors course, dispensing the most obscure Vair details known to man. Did the examiner really need to know that the final Corvair was a two-door coupe built on May 14, 1969, the 1,710,017th Corvair that GM manufactured?

I had to tip my hat to the examiner for his patience, but finally he could take no more. What sane man could? "So let's cut to the chase," he insisted. "What I'm hearing is the government said that if the tires are inflated to the manufacturer's recommendations, the car is safe, correct?"

"Yes!" said Benjy, so enthusiastically that it came out sounding like "Duh."

"So show me that the tire pressures on this car are to the manufacturer's recommendations," said the examiner. I saw he was setting a clever trap for Benjy. "If they are not, this is an unsafe car. Attempting to take the driver's road test in an unsafe car is an automatic failure of the test." Benjy protested that the examiner had misunderstood the distinction between our safe Late Model and the Early Model indicted by Nader. But the examiner held up his hand; he had heard enough. He would brook no lawyerly quibbles and technicalities. "Show me the tires are inflated to the pressures in the owner's manual," he repeated.

When I moved toward the car to retrieve our tire pressure gauge, the examiner stopped me. "Not you," he growled, jabbing his thumb toward Benjy. "Him. The applicant."

As ordered, Benjy went to the glove box and retrieved the owner's manual and our tire gauge. "It recommends fifteen pounds in the front tires and twenty-six in the rear," he said, without even opening the manual to check. "It's on page thirty-four." The examiner glowered at what he perceived as snarky impudence, but Benjy never saw it. He was too busy checking the tire pressures, just as he did each time we stopped for gas.

"Well?" said the examiner, having checked page thirty-four in the manual to confirm the recommended temperatures were just as Benjy said.

"Nineteen in each front tire and twenty-nine in each rear tire," Benjy reported.

"That's not what the manual recommends, is it?" asked the examiner, springing his trap.

It was over. Benjy's chance for a license today had just dropped from approximately to absolutely zero.

"Those recommendations are for when the car has been sitting for three hours or longer and the tires are cold," said Benjy. "The manual says that on page thirty-four. Tire pressures increase when the tires are hot. They are hot now because we drove on them and it is a hot day and they are resting on a hot surface. These tires are inflated correctly."

It was the right answer, and the examiner knew it. Benjy had avoided his trap.

"Get in the car," the examiner demanded.

Benjy purposefully strode to the driver's door, opened it, strapped himself in, and gave the examiner a tour of the car's controls. He was on his own now. And, while he had escaped the examiner's tire inflation trap, certainly there were other traps he could set that would trip Benjy up. After Benjy's eternal, tedious Corvair encomiums, there was simply no way the examiner would let him pass the test.

I could relax. I no longer had any doubt that Benjy could drive a car safely. In fact, in 30 days, he had grown into the most safety-focused driver I had ever seen. By sheer concentration, he had overcome every challenge his Asperger's presented to his competence behind the wheel. Just as important, Stan had been right; he would never, ever indulge in the driving weaknesses of normals. There would be no texting, no phoning, no radio playing, no alcohol—nothing other than a thousand percent hyper-focus on moving a Corvair safely from Point A to Point B. If I'd had a "normal" child, I'd be worried to death every time he or she got behind the wheel. But I'd ride with Benjy any time; if he was driving alone, I would not lose sleep.

Which is why I had lost so much sleep over the past week. Because it meant that something I never believed could happen, now might actually happen. I had always wanted Benjy to get his driver's license; it would be another step—a ticket—to his living independently and finding his own place in the world. But did he really need to drive a real race car? In a real race? Since that had always been impossible, I'd tried to be supportive. "Of course you'll race one day," I'd say. "There are no limits to what you can do if you try." What parent wouldn't say that? Why dash his hopes? It was like the Tooth Fairy—a harmless parental fib that a child eventually outgrows. He'd learn the truth soon enough. Why be the Bad Guy if I didn't have to?

But over the past week, as Benjy's driving became more and more proficient and the Grand Prix loomed, I had to face the very real possibility that he had actually come to that moment where dream might become reality. He might actually qualify to race a real car in a real car race—and that race was tomorrow! Sure, it wasn't a real NASCAR-style speed race. Kenny had sworn it wouldn't be like that, but what the heck did he know? He hadn't been to a Grand Prix in years; maybe it all had changed. Maybe the Grand Prix drivers today really slammed the gas pedal through the floor board and took turns on two wheels. What if something happened? Something bad? It was all happening too fast. I couldn't relax. I couldn't sleep.

But now I had the best possible outcome. Benjy would get his driver's license on his second try with a different examiner next week and be a fine, safe driver. And he would not be eligible to race tomorrow. I would sleep well tonight.

Within what seemed like a blink, Benjy was parking the Corvair directly in front of me. Perfect, I thought; he'd barely gotten out of the parking lot before the examiner flunked him. Then the examiner threw off his safety belt and hurled himself out of the car. Excellent! He couldn't get out of the Corvair fast enough to process the paperwork to fail Benjy. As he rushed past me, he muttered, "I sure wouldn't let my child drive an unsafe car."

"Neither would I," I shot back furiously. The nerve of that guy! Talking about my kid and my car like that! The examiner responded by spitting right behind me into the bushes just as the DMV office door swung shut behind him. If there had been any chance that Benjy might have passed the road test, I had just cleverly squelched it.

Fifteen minutes later, Benjy had his driver's license. "He said he wanted to flunk me, but I didn't do anything wrong," Benjy recounted to me as I pretended to seem thrilled. "And I didn't talk about Corvairs while I was driving. I didn't talk about anything. I was too busy going over my checklist. He liked my checklist. He said if I wrote it out and brought it back to him, he'd give it to other new drivers because it's a really good checklist. He thinks it should be included in the DMV training manual."

"Well, we should celebrate," I said, even though I felt like crying. I had been double-crossed by a DMV examiner who seemed so unreasonably prejudiced, yet turned out to be so scrupulously fair that he was now one of Benjy's biggest fans.

Benjy declined to go to McDonald's. We hadn't returned after we learned Lydia had been fired. Wendy's would be enjoying his patronage from now on; their Chicken Nuggets were superior, he claimed. But now he insisted we go to Kenny's. "To prepare for the race," he said.

"Stop worryin'!" Kenny exploded at me. While Benjy turned practice laps in the Deathmobile, efficiently navigating his way around the Corvairs in the field, I'd been trying to persuade Kenny that letting him race tomorrow was not a great idea. He wasn't buying it. "He'll be fine!" he shouted at me. In an old biddy's voice, he mocked: "What if this happens, what if that happens? I'm so scared." You sound like my Aunt Mildred. She worried whether the sun would rise the next day. Heck, I was younger than Benjy when I first raced!" He took a long swig of his soda, then crumpled the can and threw the empty at me. "If you don't want him to race, fine. But do you know how many people have been killed in all the years of this race? None. Do you know how many have been injured? A couple. The worst was a broken arm. I mean, come on! It's safe!"

He cracked open another soda from his suddenly alcohol-free cooler and took a long swallow. "They got a zillion rules for safety. Too many if you ask me. Like no alcohol," he said just before he burped loudly. "Even though I'm cuttin' way back. Which your boy got me to do, by the way," he said, pointing out to Benjy. "Look, we installed a safety cage in the car. We installed a safety seat in the car. He's wearing a safety suit and helmet while he's drivin' the car. They black flag anyone not drivin' safely. Heck, he'll be safer on that track than he'll be drivin' on the highway to get there." He took another big gulp of soda and belched. "I got to drive with one hand on the knob on the steering wheel and the other on the hand control for the pedals. I cain't exactly walk away from the car if there's trouble. And they're lettin' me drive. That's how safe they think it is. That's how safe I think it is."

Kenny took another big swig, crumpled the can against his forehead, then continued ripping me. "He did everything he had to do to get here. He deserves it. He earned it. And look at him! He's doin' it just right, no cowboyin' around out there. Mister Smooth. Safest driver ever. So you do your own dirty work—I don't want no part of it."

"Look, he's my son," I explained. "I'm concerned, okay? I don't want him hurt. And maybe I wonder if you're being so supportive of him racing tomorrow because you want to race. And if we drop out, you can't."

Kenny glared right through me. "Get off my land," he ordered. "And don't come to the racetrack, either of you. I'd rather not race than race with you, okay? There, you got your wish—he ain't racin'. Was that yer plan? Go on, get out of here. He's welcome anytime. But I don't want you around no more." He turned and rolled away from me.

That wasn't my plan. I didn't have a plan. All I knew was that, as I'd done with Katie, I'd said whatever popped into my head, no matter how hurtful it was, with all the sensitivity of a cinder block. "Kenny," I said, "I'm sorry. You just proved I was totally wrong and I apologize for thinking it and saying it. I just don't want to lose my son. That's all this is about. I lost my wife a couple years ago, and I can't lose my son."

Kenny kept his back to me, staring out at the field. "I don't want to lose him either," he finally said in a voice so low I could barely hear. "I know you love your kid. Well, I love that kid, too, y'know." He spun his chair to face me. "You say you don't want to lose your son. You better know that, if you don't let him race now, you will lose him."

I knew he was right.

"It's been five years, man," Kenny said, after a long silence. "Five years of hospitals and rehab and then comin' back here in this chair and feelin' like I couldn't do one single, solitary, damn thing. I don't feel that way anymore. I finished fixin' up that Deathmobile. And I'm gonna fix up and sell all them Corvairs in the field. You just watch. It'll take me ten times as long as anyone else, but that's okay, I'll do 'em ten times as good. There's still enough Corvair lovers and garbage races to run. There's money in it—there's a business. Even if there ain't, at least I won't be sittin' around doin' nothin' except feelin' sorry for myself. At least I'll be livin' again. And all that is because of that kid. Because I yelled at him, and he called me out, and he made me see what a sorry ass I'd become. He's even got me thinkin' maybe I ought to try some college, the way he carries on about it."

"That's great, Kenny, really," I said. I walked over and put my hand on his shoulder.

"I know you don't think much of me," he said, gazing out to the field. "We got off on the wrong foot. You came along at my worst time. I'm not really that bad. I'm tryin', I really am."

"I think you're good, Kenny," I said. "Really good."

We stayed like that, with my hand on Kenny's shoulder, watching Benjy, until he drove the Deathmobile over. The mannequin torsos no longer stuck out of the shark's mouth; Kenny decided they were a possible safety hazard. Benjy released himself from the straps of the seat, hopped out, and took off his helmet. "How was I?" he gushed, pumped up like a bull frog.

"Outstanding," I said, because it was true. "How's the car?"

"It runs better than ours!" Benjy crowed. "That rebuilt engine is great!"

"Those new tires I put on it help, too," said Kenny.

There was an awkward silence. Kenny eyed me, waiting for me to tell Benjy that we had to stop, that the whole idea of him racing had been a fantasy that should not become reality—at least, not tomorrow.

I couldn't do it. I wouldn't do it. Kenny was right. It was time to put the fear aside. If something terrible happened, forgive me, Annie and Benjy and Grandpa and everyone, but I just couldn't deny him. I couldn't say no.

"Well, I guess I better practice," I said. "I don't want to let you guys down tomorrow."

"Yes!" shouted Kenny, slapping his thigh with joy. "We are racing tomorrow!"

Benjy eyed us both quizzically. "Of course we are," he said.

On the western horizon, headed our way, I saw menacing thunder-bumpers that threatened to unleash a deluge. Annie, was this your work? Had I so abdicated my parental responsibility that you'd put in a word with the Higher Power to put a stop to this?

"Looks like rain coming," I said. "We might get rained out."

"Is it like NASCAR?" Benjy asked. "Do they dry the track after the rain stops, then race?"

"Heck, no," said Kenny, scanning the sky. "They ain't got no billion dollar blowers; they ain't even got towels. But that don't matter cuz it ain't gonna rain." He sounded confident. Like he'd also had a word with the Higher Power.

CHAPTER 18

The morning of the race dawned with a sky as clear and pastel blue as my father's old Corvair. Summer's usual strength-sapping, breath-stealing humidity had taken the day off. I groaned after I opened my blinds to look out the window; Kenny apparently had more pull than Annie with the Big Man and it was depressingly obvious the race would not be rained out. I trudged into Benjy's room as if my feet weighed a ton each and opened the curtains to the unwelcome sun. "Can't be late for the drivers meeting, dude," I muttered with resignation. "We need to go. Unless you want to sleep in. If you're tired. Or having second thoughts. There's no pressure to go. I'm sure Kenny will understand if you don't feel like it."

Benjy leaped out of bed, revealing that he'd slept in his clothes in order to make a faster getaway to the racetrack. After a quick breakfast, we each grabbed a handle of our cooler filled with food and sodas and hauled it out to the Corvair. As we opened the front trunk to store it, Benjy said, "Dad, there's a homeless person in the car."

Sure enough, with a dusty, decrepit coat over his head, someone was sound asleep in our Vair's back seat; in front was a garbage bag bulging with clothes and possessions. "We should call 911," Benjy said. "He may be hungry or need a doctor. Homeless people often have trouble getting the services they need. They are often discriminated against."

That may have been true, but our Corvair seemed an odd place of refuge for a homeless person. I opened the door, reached in, and gently shook the intruder.

It was Lydia. With the sun catching her flush in the eyes, she blinked herself awake. "Hi," she said lethargically, twisting herself upright. "Surprise," she added, yawning.

"Why aren't you sleeping in a bed?" Benjy demanded.

"Long story," she sighed, stretching. "So did you get your license? Still going to your race? See, I remembered! Today's the big day. I'd love to see you race. Can I go with you?"

I asked to hear Lydia's "long story." Because I suspected she was running away. And so she was, but with parental permission.

"Okay, long story short, my step-dad is a pig," she said, climbing stiffly out of the back seat. "We're always fighting, which makes my mother crazy. So I asked my real dad if I could live with him and The New Wife for at least the summer and he said okay, as long as we all get along. Except I wasn't going up there till next week. But last night, this creature my mother married got drunk...." Lydia's words came faster as she got upset. "And he yelled at me about getting fired from my job and leaving my jerk boyfriend and what a piece of trash I was. To which I said, 'Yeah, I am really sorry I lost my job; I forgot I was supporting you, and what a bummer for you—maybe now you'll have to get your own job! And I thought Bobby was such a lying loser, but you make me realize he's an absolute prince, compared to you.' So he threw a beer can at me, which he often does, except this time it was full and it hit me in the head. My mother got hysterical, and so did I, and things kinda went south after that. So I'm going to my father's a week early, and I need a ride and don't have a car or money, and he lives in West Virginia someplace. And I remembered my good friend, Benjy, was headed there to race today. So here I am. Begging for a ride, please, please, please."

"I think you should be able to live where you choose," said Benjy approvingly. "Me, too," he added with a look to me.

I cringed. "Benjy, I hope you can see that Lydia is talking about an abusive home situation, which is very, very, very different from us," I told him.

"I still should be able to live independently," he insisted.

Lydia laughed. "You see, right there, that's why I like you, Benjy. You say exactly what you're thinking, you don't play games. But, hey, you got a good thing going at home. What do you want to leave for?" She jabbed him playfully in the chest.

"Oww," he said, rubbing his chest.

"So guess what?" she went on, practically pleading. "My father said he will pick me up at the track. And at the race, to pay my way, I can be a mechanic or a cheerleader, whatever you need. Except I don't know anything about mechanics or cheerleading."

"Great!" shouted Benjy. He looked over at me, and I nodded. I was thrilled to have her join us, as long as her parents agreed.

Lydia's smile lit up her face. "Promise the wheel won't fall off again?" she asked Benjy.

"My friend Kenny is a Corvair mechanic, and he fixed it," Benjy said confidently. "It's great now." For the next 90 minutes, until we reached the racetrack, interrupted only by my phone calls to Lydia's mother and father to verify that she wasn't running away, Benjy evangelized the gospel of the Corvair to Lydia, detail by excruciating detail. I checked the rear view mirror often during the drive to see if she was bored. She appeared fascinated.

In the garage area of the Summit Point racetrack, coughing and wheezing clunkers rolled off trailers and into their assigned stalls. Disgraced, execrable nameplates like Gremlin, Pacer, and Yugo commingled with broken-down taxis and used-up police cars in an ignominious congregation of automotive donkeys that had somehow escaped the glue factory. Weird as the cars appeared when parked, in motion their bizarre paint jobs and getups made them look like a NASCAR parody. One decrepit Oldsmobile minivan had been transformed with paint and aluminum foil into a cruise missile. A team of Scandinavian Vikings wore fur loin cloths and ram's-horn helmets while working on their Fred Flintstone-ish "Saab Story." A dilapidated Cadillac hearse was rumored to be carrying a deceased visitor from a galaxy far, far away that, prior to its passing, had been held prisoner in Area 51; the race team members, heavily armed with squirt guns and peashooters, refused all comment, citing National Security.

Kenny had already arrived at our assigned stall, hauling the Deathmobile on his truck trailer. Our killer shark on wheels glittered, relatively-speaking, as most of the other racers looked no better than rolling cow pies. Kenny had polished not only our racer but himself; he'd cut and washed his hair, trimmed his beard, and put on a clean T-shirt. Returning to the race he'd missed for five years, he positively glowed.

We introduced Kenny to Lydia, and his glow went supernova. "You dog, you!" he teased Benjy. "You didn't tell me you had a lady friend."

Benjy blushed, turning as purple as when Kenny's dogs attacked him. For one of the few times in his life, he was speechless.

"Whatever," Lydia laughed, putting her arm around Benjy, who not only didn't flinch, but smiled. Separated from her stepfather by 90 miles, she glowed almost as brightly as Kenny, and reveled in the Grand Prix's silly zeitgeist. "This is totally goofy cool," she exulted.

Just then, four Vikings from the Saab Story team ambushed Kenny, blew a ram's horn in his ear, and hoisted him onto their shoulders. "Dad, they're kidnapping Kenny!" Benjy cried out.

"I think they're old friends," I said, seeing the social cue of elation on Kenny's face. "Very old friends." As the Vikings paraded Kenny through the garage, more and more very old friends of Kenny from races run long ago engulfed him, welcoming him back like a long-lost member of their zany tribe. Word spread through the pits; soon, the crowd of racers and crew members passed him around on their shoulders, cheering. He was home again, and he was happy.

While Kenny renewed old friendships, we headed to the office to register for the race. Before we could enter, our way was blocked by one of the race officials, wearing a long black robe, an Olde English powdered wig, and a monocle, who demanded to see Benjy's driver's license. "I say," he intoned in a hopelessly phony English accent, "you're a tad young, are you not? Render your license! Forthwith!" Startled, Benjy nervously handed over the temporary paper license he'd received from the DMV. "I say!" cried the official again, his eyes widening and his monocle dropping to his chest. "You've had a license to drive for one day! Twenty-four hours! Odds bodkins!" He lifted his monocle back to his eye and peered accusingly through it at Benjy. Four other judges, all wearing powdered wigs, robes, and monocles, promenaded over as if they were royalty. Each inspected the license closely, as if it might be a fake, while murmuring "odds bodkins!"—they looked and sounded like a waddle of penguins.

Alarmed, Benjy asked, "What does 'odds bodkins' mean? Is it bad?"

Reverting to his native Texas accent, the first judge said, "I have no idea what it means, kid. But are you sure you know how to drive?"

"Yes. I'm a very good driver." Even with the judge's fake accent gone, betraying the joke, Benjy was anxious.

"Have you ever raced?" the judge haughtily demanded, back in his hammy English accent.

"Yes," Benjy answered. "In video games."

"Do not be clever or evasive with the Almightiest Judge of the Grand Prix du Garbage," the judge chastised him. "You have never raced, is the true testimony! What kind of car are you driving?"

"A Chevrolet Corvair." The judge gasped, staggered, and grabbed his chest as if having a heart attack, so Benjy quickly added, "But it's a Late Model. Which is not the kind that Ralph Nader—"

"SILENCE!" cried the judge, raising his hand, suddenly fully recovered from his cardiac troubles. And Benjy silenced—instantly. "I know it well," the judge growled. "You're really making it hard for me, the Almightiest Judge of the Grand Prix du Garbage, to let you race, when you are a new driver who has never raced and who is driving a car that is"—he then bitterly spit out the hated words—"UNSAFE AT ANY SPEED!"

"That is not true!" Benjy protested.

"You will at all times address the Almightiest Judge of the Grand Prix du Garbage as Your Honor!"

"Yes, sir," said Benjy.

"YES, YOUR HONOR!" bellowed the judge.

Benjy turned pale and looked to me for help. That this judge's performance was all part of the silliness of the race had eluded him. So I winked to clue him in on the joke, but that may have eluded him as well.

"What were you sputtering about this unworthy car?" His Honor continued. "This Exhibit A of American corporate irresponsibility? This DEATHMOBILE?!"

"It's not, Your Honor," Benjy managed, still uncertain if this inquisition was real.

"Yet you name it 'The Deathmobile' right here in your racing application!" cried His Honor, punching his clipboard with a list of entries. "An admission of guilt! I rest my case!"

Benjy was on the verge of tears. "But that's a joke, Your Honor. That is called 'irony.' Because it's not really a Death—"

"SILENCE!" His Honor again demanded. He brought his face close to Benjy's so that their noses nearly touched. "Do I look like I'm laughing at this so-called irony? You may have come a long way for nothing, Young Whippersnapper!"

Benjy went mute. He feared his racing career was over before it started. Then His Honor leaned down and quietly whispered, "Young Man, this is all a pose I must adopt in order to protect my true identity. You see, I too am a Friend of Ed. As in Edward N. Cole."

Benjy brightened at the mention of the name of the Father of the Corvair.

"Mine is a 1969 Monza, serial number 5977," His Honor hissed.

Benjy's eyes widened. "Out of only six thousand built in 1969?!"

"Manufactured at the Willow Run, Michigan, plant on May 13, 1969, the day before production of the Greatest Car officially and permanently ended."

"Really?!" Benjy exclaimed. Then he quickly added, "Your Honor!"

"I'd have driven it here, but it broke a fan belt last night. Didn't feel like fixing it."

"Wow!" Benjy looked at me—the Champion Fan Belt Breaker—in a new light.

"You are among friends," His Honor quietly purred. "Now give me your hand so you too may be a Friend of Ed's in the Corvair Brotherhood." His Honor took Benjy's hand in his and solemnly intoned: "From this day to the ending of the world, But we in it shall be remembered. We few, we happy few, we band of brothers."

"Shakespeare wrote that," recognized Benjy.

"SILENCE! IMPUDENT SWINE!" cried His Honor. "I composed it!"

"It's from *Henry the Fifth*," added Benjy, determined to set the record straight.

The Almighty Judge again peered through his monocle at Benjy, then hissed, "Now, you impertinent young lad, listen carefully as I tell you the parable of the Tortoise and the Hare. You will be the tortoise in this race. You will drive carefully and safely. You will not go off the course. You will preserve your Corvair and finish the race. You will not permit your Corvair to come in contact with any of the second-rate automotive riff-raff cluttering up the track. Your mission is not to win the race, so do not try to win the race. Your mission is to finish in the top third—a very respectable finish for your first time—which will only be possible if you preserve your Corvair and drive it safely. Remember, at least half of those boring water pumpers out there will break down before the race ends, so, if you finish, you, the tortoise, will beat all those hares. This shall be your challenge and your quest. This shall be your triumph. As a new Friend of Ed, you will bring honor to the Corvair and those who cherish it. The Almightiest Judge of the Grand Prix du Garbage has decreed it. Do you understand my charge to you, My Brother?"

"Yes, Your Honor."

"Do you agree to obey my charge to you at all times and in all ways? So help you, God?"

"Yes, Your Honor."

"And you will ensure that Kenny and this old man and this delightful young maiden with the purple, orange, and lime hair will also obey?"

"Yes, Your Honor!"

"Do not risk my wrath by failing me. Do not speed excessively or spin out or drive too aggressively or otherwise try any funny business. I will personally black flag you and put you in our Bad Driver Dungeon. Believe me, you do not want to go there. You do not want to risk my wrath!"

"No, Your Honor!"

"My Brother—Young Man—Godspeed to you. Go out there and

make us proud." The Almightiest Judge of the Grand Prix du Garbage offered his hand to Benjy.

"Yes, Your Honor!" Benjy swore, firmly shaking His Honor's hand.

Dismissing his new charge, the Almightiest Judge turned and winked to me.

Meanwhile, Benjy stood transfixed, eyes wide.

He had heard a calling.

CHAPTER 19

After Benjy strapped himself into the Deathmobile's safety seat, I gave his shoulder harness an extra strong yank just to be certain it was secure.

"Dad, I can't breathe," he gasped. "Too tight."

"Tortoise," I insisted as I slightly loosened the belt. "You're a tortoise, not a hare!"

"Dad?"

"What?"

"It's practice laps. There are only a few other cars out there."

I sighed. Seeing the giddy goofiness of the cars, drivers, and crews, I thought I had relaxed. But now Benjy was strapped into the race car, the race would soon become real, and all my worries and fears were back in spades. "Just be careful out there," I finally said.

"I will."

I handed him the radio headset and he attached it to his helmet. "We'll call you on the radio if we want you to slow down or come into the pit, okay? And whatever the pit says is law. Period."

"We practiced that, Dad."

"If the radio doesn't work, we've got the signs and flags to communicate. Right? And you'll watch the track officials for their flags too. Right?"

"We learned all that at the drivers meeting, Dad."

"And you'll talk to us on the radio if anything goes wrong. Right?"

"Dad," Benjy sighed, "I want to practice and we've talked about this ten billion times."

He was exaggerating wildly, of course; we'd actually gone over it only about nine billion times. "Just be careful out there," I repeated. "I love you. I don't want anything to happen."

"I know," Benjy said. He turned the key and the Corvair's engine came to life, ringing and whining. Under his breath, he repeated to himself his checklist. He scanned his mirrors, dropped the Powerglide transmission lever into Drive, released the parking brake, glanced back over his shoulder, pulled out onto pit road, stopped at the exit to get clearance from the official, and then merged onto the racetrack. Like he'd done it a thousand times.

"Take it easy, Aunt Mildred," Kenny said to me. "He'll be fine."

"Look, I can't help it," I vented, talking way too fast. "I'm his father, he's my son. So quit calling me Aunt Mildred and quit telling me to stop worrying. It makes me worry even more."

"Just chill out, man!" said Kenny, raising his hands in surrender. "It's not like you're sendin' him off to war. Let's just have some fun, okay?"

"I definitely vote for fun," Lydia seconded.

"Don't encourage either Kenny or Benjy," I replied to her pointedly. When she thought I wasn't looking, she eyed Kenny and threw up her hands in bewilderment.

I moved away from both of them to the other end of our pit stall and trained my binoculars on Benjy. He was up to speed and maneuvering through Summit Point's S-curves. On my practice laps, I'd slowed the Deathmobile to a crawl and still managed to bounce it over the track's raised curbs. But on each S-curve, Benjy smoothly handled the entry and exit.

"He's done half a lap, and I can already see he's a better driver than you," Kenny shouted at me over the roar of the practice cars passing by. "We won't measure his lap times in hours."

"I set a good example for him! And you!" I shouted back.

I saw Kenny call Benjy on the radio headset. Whatever Benjy said in reply, it made Kenny cackle.

I came back over. "What?"

"He said, 'For every rookie driver, there's a first time for everything,'" Kenny reported. "What the heck does that mean?"

I knew that phrase by heart, and my knees got rubbery. He was reciting his NASCAR racing video game monologue. Reciting was one thing, but what if he really started racing that way, fender to fender with Denny Hamlin, while trying to *keep from dying at Talladega*? That settled it. The heck with what Kenny and Lydia and even Benjy thought of me; I had to watch him like a hawk. If his tortoise turned into a hare for even a second, I was pulling the plug.

As the pace car—a Pleistocene-era tow truck—pulled off into the pit lane, the 66 cars that managed to drag themselves onto the asphalt track took the green flag, and the Grand Prix du Garbage was underway. The crowd of nearly a hundred cheered wildly as the cheap racers accelerated in an ear-splitting roar, thanks to dozens of broken mufflers. The lead car, courtesy of a lucky pick in the lottery, was supposed to be the Smoking Butt, a vintage Volkswagen microbus transformed by paint and plastic into a rolling cigarette. But before it even reached the starting line it was in fact smoking from its butt; coughing badly, the Butt pulled into the infield. Stop Childhood Obesity—a Plymouth minivan transformed into a giant rolling Twinkie that had been riddled with machine gun fire—took the lead.

In our pit, waiting for Kenny to drive the Deathmobile across the starting line, Benjy quickly did some math. "Eighty cars were entered. Fourteen never made it to the starting line. That means we can't finish worse than sixty-sixth place!"

"The Smoking Butt's out!" Lydia shouted gleefully. Indeed, the Pleistocene wrecker was already preparing to haul the stricken VW back to the garage. "Don't you know smoking is bad for you?!" she jeered at the Butt's pit crew, a few stalls away from us. She was ecstatic—until she saw Benjy's ashen face. "What's the matter?" she cried. "We haven't even started and we're already up to sixty-fifth!"

"The Volkswagen is the only other car in the race besides ours with an air-cooled rear-mounted engine," Benjy fretted. "And it broke down before it even started."

Just then, after drawing a dismal 77th starting position in the lottery, Kenny urged our Corvair across the start. A round of cheers rose up from the grandstands and pits as the fans recognized him. He waved, and gave us a thumbs up while passing our pit stall.

"GO, KENNY!" Lydia screamed, jumping and kicking. "GO!"

Benjy stuck his fingers in his ears. "You're louder than the cars!" he complained to her.

"I can't help it!" Lydia giggled, punching him playfully. "I always wanted to be a cheerleader! Don't tell anyone!"

Fifty minutes later, Benjy held up our pit sign signaling Kenny to come into the pits to change drivers. But Kenny flew past, ignoring him, just as he'd ignored him for the past 10 laps. "He won't come in!" Benjy shouted at me. "The schedule says we were supposed to change drivers twenty minutes ago!"

Not only was Kenny staying out on the track, ignoring our agreed schedule of driver changes, but he was also racing like the Hare from Hell when we'd all agreed to drive like a tortoise. The Almightiest Judge of the Grand Prix du Garbage delivered the official standings to our pit, and they showed Kenny now in 24th place. In less than an hour, he'd moved the Deathmobile up 42 places. "What if a Corvair actually won one of these fiascos?" asked His Honor giddily, suddenly forgetting all his cautionary talk about being a tortoise.

It was mind-boggling. With the Corvair's small engine and an automatic transmission, Kenny gave up ground to nearly every other car on the straightaways. But in the corners, he reeled every other car back in and then left many in his dust. Entering a turn, he ducked inside the other cars, tight to the inside, barely twitching the wheel and sacrificing no speed. Exiting, with the Corvair's heavy rear end anchoring the car to the pavement, he punched the accelerator while everyone else was still braking, exploding past cars that had no idea he was even in the same corner. The Corvair was riding on rails, effortlessly working its way toward the lead.

In other words, he was setting the worst possible example for Benjy. Turning my back on Benjy and Lydia so they couldn't hear me, I called up Kenny over the radio. "What are you doing out there?!" I demanded.

"I'm racin'," he said. "What're you doin'?" Real snarky.

"We agreed to change drivers every half hour."

"Dang, my watch stopped," he drawled. "Eat some Corvair dust, Twinkie!" he cackled as he passed the Stop Childhood Obesity minivan. "It's low-fat!" With its front-wheel drive and front engine layout, the Twinkie waddled obesely into the corners and had fallen out of the lead.

"You left your mike open and I heard that," I fumed. "You're setting a fine example for Benjy. What about driving like a tortoise? What about switching drivers after half an hour?"

"Damn mike keeps sticking open," Kenny said, flicking his talk button on and off to unstick it; static sizzled in my ear like machine gun fire. He waved to us as he passed the pit, yet again ignoring Benjy's sign ordering a pit stop, then came back on the radio. "Look, I'm thinkin' Benjy should drive next."

"No," I said, then slowly repeated our pre-agreed plan. "I will drive the second shift to see what it's like before he goes out."

"Yeah, well, like they said in Iraq, the battle plan is always excellent—until the first shot's fired." With the mike stuck open again, I could again hear his cackle. "Look, for him, it'll be a piece of cake," Kenny continued. "You, on the other hand—I'm afraid you'll wreck the car. Or break it. Then he wouldn't get his chance to drive today and that would just kill him."

"I'm not going to wreck or break the car," I protested.

"All I'm sayin' is, he and I got the talent for drivin' this Corvair, and you don't, and we all know it. He races next, then you."

I was silent. I didn't know for certain if Benjy was that talented a driver; he hadn't yet turned a lap in a real race. But as much as it hurt to admit it, I did know for certain that I was not a talented driver. The racer's instincts of when to press hard into a turn, what line to take, where to start and stop braking: I had none of them. Just watching our practice laps, Kenny had seen that Benjy had the monopoly on racing talent in our family. Now he was calling me on it.

"Well?" Kenny asked, setting up the Saab Story for a pass through the S-curves. He swung wide around the last S-curve and left the Vikings in the Fred Flintstone-mobile behind. "You drive like Betty Rubble!" he mocked.

"Benjy won't want to change the order," I argued. "He can be pretty rigid."

"Tell him it's captain's orders. He'll understand."

The Alien-bearing hearse from Area 51 had just pulled into the pits with steam billowing up from underneath. That moved the Deathmobile up to almost 20th position. More than 30 cars had dropped out, and traffic had thinned out considerably. The racing looked a lot easier.

"Kenny," I said. "He will be a tortoise. He will not be trying to win this race. Right?"

"Whatever," moaned Kenny. "We could win it. Piece of cake."

"This is important to me, Kenny. It's not a joke. He's not trying to win."

"He's not trying to win," Kenny conceded. "I'm not trying to win. We will not win. Are you happy?"

"Okay," I conceded at last. "Bring it in."

"Roger that," said Kenny.

"Benjy!" I shouted, waving at him to come over from the pit wall. "You're driving next!"

He came over, eyeing me questioningly. "The plan is for you to drive next," he said.

"Kenny's the captain and this is his order," I explained, peeling off the safety suit we were sharing. "We're a team, we gotta be flexible, and we gotta follow the captain's orders."

"I don't know," said Benjy, un-persuaded. The idea of changing the driving order had thrown him a dozen curve balls all at once.

"Benjy," said Lydia, putting a soothing hand on his shoulder. "When the manager at McDonald's gave me an order, I had to follow it. Right? Or else, I got fired. That's the way it works when the captain of the team gives an order. You have to follow it."

He couldn't resist her. "Right," he finally said. "Okay."

Lydia helped him wriggle into the tight safety suit. As Kenny eased the Deathmobile into our pit stall and shut it off, I rolled his chair over to the car.

"He ain't ready yet?" Kenny groused, sliding into his chair from the safety seat. "Man, this'll be the slowest pit stop in the history of the automobile. We'll fall back twenty places!"

"We aren't winning," I reminded him testily. "We don't care about winning!"

"Yeah, yeah, yeah," Kenny mocked. "A guy cain't have fun anymore." Then he heard the ovation for him from the fans in the grandstand and the other race teams in the pits. He took off his helmet and bowed, beaming. Then he needled the crew in the pit next to ours that was fueling up the Fuzz Ball, their salvage police car. "We don't need no stinkin' gas," Kenny teased. "We're gettin' great gas mileage and still blowin' yer doors off!"

Kenny signaled me to lean down so he could speak softly. "I think I sold those Fuzz Ball guys a Corvair. For real. They talked to me about it before the race." He gestured to me to come closer and his voice grew so soft, I could barely hear it over the roar from the track. "When I got back from Iraq," he said, "and I was in the hospital, and the days were bad, the physical therapist would tell me to imagine what my best day ever would be like, because one day, if I did the rehab, I would live it. This is not that day. This is a better day. So I really don't care where we finish. Because I already won." He paused, then asked softly, "But don't tell Benjy, okay? Let him race like it means something. He'll have more fun that way."

I desperately wanted Benjy to be a tortoise, but I couldn't resist Kenny's plea. As Benjy climbed over the wall, his helmet, gloves, and safety suit finally on, I nodded my agreement. "Move your tail, Kid!" Captain Kenny ordered gruffly. "We got a race to run!"

"Yes, sir!" Benjy opened the door and buckled himself into the safety seat while I reviewed with him an endless stream of cautions he'd now heard over nine billion times. Nodding intently, he adjusted his seat and mirrors, murmuring his pre-drive checklist.

"Radio check," I ordered.

"Benjy to pit!" came through loud and clear in my headset.

With no more cautions to give, I had nothing left to say except, "Fire it up." The Deathmobile started eagerly.

"I love you, Benjy," I said.

"Okay," he replied.

I stepped back as he checked his mirror a final time, put the

Powerglide in Drive, and cautiously nosed the Deathmobile out of the pit like a turtle sticking its head out of its shell.

"Be a tortoise!" I shouted after him. Kenny glared at me. "I can't help it," I told him.

"Rock and roll, Benjy!" Lydia screamed at the top of her lungs. "Woo woo! Put that hammer down!"

I glared at her. "We're driving like a tortoise, remember?"

"Sorry," she apologized. "Closet wannabe cheerleader." She didn't sound very sorry.

Kenny intently watched Benjy merge the Deathmobile onto the track ahead of the Fuzz Ball. "Great," he moaned, sensing trouble. "That cop car is on his tail, they got a cop car engine, and they're heading to the S-curves." He grabbed the radio headset from me and put it on.

Through my binoculars, I saw Benjy give way ahead of the S-curves and let the Fuzz Ball pass him and open up a long lead. But in the curves, it had to brake hard as it wallowed from side to side. Meanwhile, Benjy confidently glided the Deathmobile through the turns, maintaining his speed so that he was soon right back on the Fuzz Ball's tail. "That was good, guiding him on how to handle that police car," I said to Kenny.

"I didn't say a word to him," Kenny replied. "He did it himself." He winked at Lydia, who hopped from one foot to the other, craned her neck, and ran up and down along the pit wall to watch every second of Benjy's drive.

In the back straightaway now, the Fuzz Ball used its gargantuan cop car V-8 to pull away from the Deathmobile. But entering the tight bus-stop turns, where the cars had to almost stop to go around a bus shelter, the cop car had to brake early and hard. Benjy stayed close, then in the last corner ducked low and inside as the Fuzz Ball's bulk forced it out wide until it was nearly off the track and into the grass.

"HE PASSED THE FUZZ BALL!" Lydia exploded, jumping and spinning in the air. "Take that, you Big Fat Energy Hog!" She high-fived Kenny, then tried to high-five me as well, but held back when she saw my glare.

"Sorry," she apologized again. "I just can't help it. Aren't you excited?!"

"You're fine," I said. "I'm just not there yet."

"WELL, I AM!" she blasted, turning back to the track and cheering wildly as Benjy left the Fuzz Ball behind and took aim at his next pass—the alien-bearing Area 51 hearse now back on the track after pit repairs. "Eat that alien up, Benjy! Balls to the Wall!"

"Lydia!" I shouted.

"Let him alone," she barked back to me. "Let. Him. Go."

I glared at her. Hard. And she glared right back. Finally, I turned away from her to watch Benjy drive. Fortunately, he wasn't hearing Lydia's shouts, because he wasn't driving Balls to the Wall to pass Area 51. Instead, he bided his time. For one, two, then three laps, he brought the Deathmobile past our pit, stalking the Alien hearse. He drove modestly, even stolidly, yet on each lap he gained a few precious car lengths. Like a pro, he was setting the hearse up for a pass.

Something was wrong, though. I wasn't sure what, but, each time the Deathmobile passed our pit, I knew something was very, very wrong.

I looked over to the grandstands where the crowd was hanging on Benjy's methodical pursuit of the hearse, cheering him on. "Deathmobile!" saluted the partying fans, hoisting beer cups as Benjy flew past, gaining on the hearse. If only they'd known how we got here: that, just a few months earlier, Benjy wouldn't or couldn't get out of bed after his college rejection; he wouldn't go to the DMV to apply for a driver's license because he was certain he'd be rejected; the only racing he'd ever done was in his video game; he had no friends. And then he let a "different, but not disabled" car enter his life. And that car had changed everything.

"DEATHMOBILE!" the crowd roared again as Benjy finished another lap, now just two car lengths behind the hearse.

Yes, something was very wrong. And I had to put a stop to it. "Let me talk to him," I said to Kenny, holding my hand out for the radio.

"You can't," replied Kenny. "The mike is stuck open again."

"Is he talking?"

Kenny shrugged evasively. He reluctantly surrendered the headset.

"Don't get all Aunt Mildred about it. He's driving incredible."

I put on the headset and listened.

Stalking the Area 51 Alien-Bearing Hearse down the back straightaway at Summit Point, Benjy Bennett, the talented rookie who has taken the Grand Prix by storm, knew the hearse was loose. It seemed to want to roll over in every turn.

Still, Benjy was part of a team and he had strict orders. He was the tortoise in this race. But it's the tortoise that eventually wins the race, not the hare, so at some point the tortoise must pass the hare. That time had come. It was time for the tortoise to make his move.

There would be no nudging. There would be no swapping paint. This was not some kid playing a video game. No, the New Kid on the Block knew the difference between luck and skill, and he couldn't rely on luck anymore; there was only his skill. He would have to outthink and outdrive the hearse and everyone else on the track today.

Benjy was now on the bumper of the hearse as he passed the pit again, and again the crowd cheered him on. At the end of the S-curves, he made his move. The hearse had carried too much speed into the final curve and had to lock up and smoke its brakes to stay on course. Benjy held his speed and easily slid by. He'd patiently waited for the hearse to give him his opportunity, and he'd taken it.

"DEATHMOBILE!" thundered the crowd after he pulled ahead of the hearse. And as Benjy roared past the grandstand, Lydia became the cheerleader she'd always wanted to be, leading the fans chanting, "DEATHMOBILE! DEATHMOBILE! DEATHMOBILE!"

Every bone in my body said all this was wrong, terribly wrong. As I heard Benjy plot his next pass into the open mike, I removed the headset. I had seen and heard enough. His talking to himself sounded so appropriate, such a welcome change from the same reciting I'd heard every morning for the past five years. And he was driving responsibly, even beautifully. That only strengthened my resolve. I had to take action.

Kenny saw my misgivings. "It's harmless," he said. "He talks to himself. Don't make a big deal out of it. Just let him race. He's a natural."

I handed Kenny the head set, then marched to the pit wall and held up our sign ordering Benjy to pit. A half mile ahead of the Alien hearse now, he saw the sign as he passed and gave a puzzled thumbs up, even though the stop wasn't on the schedule.

"He wants to know why he has to come in," Kenny relayed from the radio.

"Tell him it's because his mike is stuck," I shouted to be heard over the engines.

"I cain't tell him his mike is stuck when his mike is stuck! Ben, just cuz he's reciting is no reason to pull him in. We don't need the radio. Most teams don't even have radios."

"He's doing great!" Lydia shouted at me. "He's not doing anything wrong! Why do you have to ruin it for him?"

Kenny put his hand on Lydia's arm to calm her down.

"I am his father," I said tersely. "I don't need to explain or justify anything to either of you."

Kenny and Lydia threw up their hands—I was a jerk, ruining everything.

"Look, this is important to me," I tried to explain. "It's between Benjy and me. I don't expect you to understand." I left them and walked over to the pit wall.

Following race rules to the letter, Benjy slowed to a safe speed and eased his way down pit road, then expertly turned into our stall. He shifted the car to neutral, pulled up the parking brake, turned off the engine, and hopped out of the car. "What's wrong, Dad?" he shouted at me.

With a can of black paint that I'd found in Kenny's tool chest, I hopped over the pit wall and completely sprayed over the "Death" in Deathmobile on Benjy's door. I hated that word. I never wanted to hear it again.

Above where I'd painted over "Death," I wrote "Life."

"From now on, we're driving the Lifemobile," I informed Benjy. "Is that clear?"

"Okay," said Benjy. He eyed me as if I'd lost my mind.

"Now get back out there and race," I ordered. "Carefully."

Benjy didn't wait for me to change my mind. He hopped back in the car and had pulled onto Pit Lane before I realized I'd forgotten to tell him to unstick his mike button. But it didn't matter. He didn't need my help out there.

I walked back over to Kenny and Lydia.

Lydia nodded, slowly raising her hand for a high five, and I gladly slapped it.

Kenny offered his hand, and I shook it. He held on, then pulled me down into an embrace. He was crying.

CHAPTER 20

The cemetery's grass was freshly cut; not a blade raised its head over Annie's or Dad's flat, simple grave markers. That impressed me— the management had no notice that I was coming. After the Grand Prix had ended, and we'd put the Lifemobile back on Kenny's trailer for the ride home, the summer solstice sun was still high. We had- n't won the race, of course, but we'd finished a very respectable 14th, still running strong as the checkered flag waved. The Almightiest Judge of the Grand Prix du Garbage was so ecstatic that he shook up a bottle of beer, sprayed it all over Kenny, and then came out of the closet, pub- licly proclaiming himself a Corvair-loving, Corvair-owning Friend of Ed. During the revelry, my thoughts had turned to Annie and Dad; they would have rejoiced in Benjy's triumphant day. The cemetery wasn't far from the racetrack and it was on the way to Lydia's father's house. So here I was.

The first time I'd come here, I had buried Dad while still fuming about the sharp salesman that had him buy these family plots when he wasn't thinking clearly. The next—and last—time I had visited, I buried Annie. So I never had fond feelings for the place. But now, as the sun set over the Appalachian Mountains, with the grass pristine and the manager patiently waiting for me at the gate, albeit after I'd slipped him $20, I found the place growing on me. Maybe, when Dad bought these plots, he knew exactly what he was doing.

In the parking area below the graves, Benjy paced in a circle, furi- ously reciting, flapping his hand, still flying high from the exhilaration of his first race. I'd tried to persuade him to come with me up the hill to the graves. "No, thanks," he insisted. A few months earlier, I might have insisted right back, loudly, that he join me, that it was his duty as a son and grandson. A shouting match might have erupted. But now I accepted his decision. Of course, having Lydia glare at me, silently telling me to let Benjy make up his own mind, was also persuasive.

From atop the hill, I watched them; as Benjy paced, Lydia leaned against our Corvair and chatted with him, her eyes following him back and forth as if she were watching a tennis match. We'd butted heads a lot today, but Benjy was crazy about her, and she had been so wonderfully supportive of him. We both wished she wasn't moving away.

Although what happened next made me wonder if she was too supportive of him.

"Still wired from the race?" I asked Benjy when I returned to the car.

"Yeah," he admitted. "I can't wait to do it again." He stopped pacing. Then he said, "Dad?"

"Yes?"

"Mom and Granddad aren't alive anymore. So when you were up there, you were only talking to yourself. They can't hear you. You always tell me not to talk to myself."

"You're right," I confessed. "But, standing there at their graves, I thought, what the heck, if they can hear me and I don't talk out loud, what a waste of time it was coming here. Or maybe I was just talking to myself. I don't know."

"Dead people can't hear, Dad," he pressed. "So I don't see why we had to come here. You can talk to yourself at home. We didn't have to come to a cemetery. I don't like cemeteries. They're just full of decomposing dead bodies."

I eyed Lydia. "Is this what you were discussing while I was up there?"

She shrugged innocently. "Among other things."

"Yes," Benjy confirmed, resuming his pacing. "Since you were up there talking to yourself for so long."

"Well, here's what I took so long to say up there, in case you're interested. I told them that the Almighty Judges of the Grand Prix du Garbage unanimously chose you as their Rookie of the Year and gave you that big trophy in the back of the car. And I told them that you passed your driver's test in our Corvair. Your Grandpa would jump out of the grave and do back flips if he heard that. And I told Mom that you made two friends, Kenny and Lydia. She would love hearing that. And I told them that, after working unbelievably hard to pass your math assessment, you're going to college, and that someday in the future I have no doubt you will live independently, just like you've always wanted. And I told them how incredibly proud I am of you and all you've accomplished, and all you will accomplish tomorrow and the next day and the day after that. And that I wish they were here to see it all, to experience the same love and joy and pride that I'm feeling right now."

"But they aren't there in the dirt," Benjy insisted. "So you could have told them at home." He was not what you might call "sentimental."

"Benjy," Lydia chided, "you're missing the point. Your dad was complimenting you. It was nice. And appropriate. Give it a rest."

"It still seems like a double standard," Benjy complained. "You shouldn't talk to yourself, Dad. That's the rule for everyone."

"I won't anymore," I pledged. "One rule for everyone."

"So now tell him what you told me," Lydia urged Benjy.

He firmly shook his head no.

"What?" I prodded.

Benjy hesitated. "Mom should have gotten a flu shot," he said finally. "They were only twenty dollars at the pharmacy. I saw other moms get them."

"I wish she had, too," I said. "I really, really wish she had. Because I miss her so much."

Suddenly turning purple, Benjy erupted into tears. I reached to embrace him, but he refused, wriggling away from my touch. "It's okay to cry," I told him. "I'm crying, too."

Soon, Benjy announced, "I'm okay. I'm fine." He wiped his eyes with his sleeve.

"We've been talking about a lot of stuff," Lydia said. "As you can see."

I wiped my eyes on my sleeve and looked to Benjy. "Is there more you want to say?"

He shook his head no.

"Say it," Lydia encouraged him.

"What?" I asked. "She's right. You can tell me."

Benjy's chin dropped to his chest. Finally, he said, "Grandpa wanted me to go to Dartmouth College, and I didn't. I failed to go there."

I was relieved this was about something so relatively minor. I smiled. "Benjy, that was a long time ago. Please don't worry about it. That's when he wasn't thinking clearly. It became obvious that was not the best place for you, and Grandpa would have agreed with that, I'm certain. He did for me. The important thing is Grandpa wanted you to go to college, and you're going to college. So he'd be very proud."

Then I saw Lydia gesture to Benjy to keep talking. I realized there was more, and it was serious.

"I don't want to go to college, Dad," he said.

After a moment, I managed to say, "Oh."

"I mean, I want to go to college, but—" His voice trailed off. He looked to Lydia, and she made a gesture, encouraging him to plunge ahead. Benjy fixed his eyes on mine. "I only want to take the courses I want, not the ones they want. I want to study English and history and political science and psychology. And car repair. So I can fix Corvairs like Kenny."

"That's—wow—that's a big change from your plan," I said. I eyed Lydia, wondering what she might have had to do with this; she shrugged as if to say she was blameless. "Benjy, you won't get your college diploma that way," I said. "There are certain courses you need to take, even if you don't like them. That's just the way the system works."

"But that doesn't make sense to me."

"I know," I confessed. "It doesn't make sense to me either. But that's the way it is."

"I want to learn about what I'm interested in while I work on Corvairs with Kenny. That's what I want to do now—work on Corvairs with Kenny."

"Do you mean work on Corvairs with Kenny as a job? A career?" I sighed a very loud sigh.

Benjy nodded eagerly, despite my clear social cue of disappointment.

I again turned to Lydia to see if she'd instigated this. She raised her hands innocently. "Don't look at me. It's what he told me while you were up there. It's what he wants."

"Wow, Benjy, this is a lot," I sputtered. "This needs to be thought through very carefully. Ver-ry carefully. We've had a lot of excitement today. Let's take a day or two to digest all this."

Benjy didn't want to wait a day or two. "I want to go to college and study what I want, and work on Corvairs with Kenny, and earn money when we sell them," he said softly. "He says we can be partners, and it'll be a good business. Lydia said she'll buy a Corvair from us, and two other people at the race want one, so we've made three sales already."

I turned to Lydia again. "When I earn enough to buy a car," she said, pushing a purple lock out of her eyes, "it'll be one of Benjy's Corvairs. Because I know it'll be a good car."

"Yes," said Benjy, emphatically.

"I think this all sounds cool," said Lydia. "Really, really cool."

I didn't think it sounded cool. I liked Lydia a lot, but I was very happy to see her father pull into the parking area to take her away. Parking several spots away, he waved dourly to us; he didn't seem overjoyed to be there. "Pop the trunk," Lydia called to him as she retrieved her garbage bag of belongings from our Corvair. She hurled the bag in the open trunk, slammed the lid shut, then returned to us.

"So. Long day, huh?" she said to Benjy.

"All days are 24 hours long," Benjy replied.

Lydia grinned and tried to pull Benjy into an embrace. Benjy held his arms by his side and stiffened. "It's okay to hug, isn't it?" she asked. "You can put your arms around me, can't you?" She slowly raised first his left arm and then his right. "You're practically an adult now, so you can do this," she instructed. "And then you bring your hands against my back and squeeze a little. Not too hard. Just enough. And I do the same to you."

He let his fingers extend slowly to touch the back of her shirt, then gently squeezed.

"Perfect," she said quietly as she relaxed for a moment in his arms. "Even though I don't know you that well, Benjy, you're like the only person in the world I trust. And even though I'm going away, I want to stay in touch with you, okay? I want to hear how you're doing, and tell you how I'm doing. And I want to see you when I come back to see my mom. Will you promise to stay in touch with me?"

"Okay," Benjy agreed. "I'm going to learn how to use Facebook."

"Then I'm going to friend you," Lydia replied.

"Great," Benjy said proudly. "You'll be my first friend."

"Well, I can't keep the old man waiting." Just as Lydia had raised his arms to begin their embrace, now she lowered them to end it. Then she kissed him on the cheek. "I love you, Benjy," she said softly.

"Okay," he said.

"When someone says that, it's nice to say 'I love you' back. If you mean it."

Benjy nodded. He understood. Finally, he said, "I love you."

Pleased, Lydia turned to me. "Don't take it so hard, Mister B," she said as she walked backwards to her father's car. "It'll all work out somehow."

"Goodbye, Lydia," I said, hoping she was right.

She got into the passenger seat of her father's car, and they were quickly gone.

"She's quite a girl," I told Benjy. "I can see why you like her."

His chin was on his chest.

"She'll be back to see us," I said. "You'll be friends a long time."

"Dad?" he asked.

"Yes."

"I want to live at Kenny's house," he said.

I sighed loudly again, and looked away to the sunset over the mountains.

"Upstairs—the upstairs of Kenny's house," he emphasized.

"I heard you, Benjy, it's just a lot to process at once. You're making my head spin." I sighed and walked in a circle to digest this. "But what about those dogs?" I said finally. "You don't like those dogs. Benjy, you— I mean—living with Kenny. I mean, he's Kenny. Right?" I couldn't even form a sentence.

"I think I'm okay with the dogs now that they know me. And Kenny's my friend, even if you don't like him. We would be like a team.

I can help him do things he can't do. And he can help me do things I can't do. We'll rebuild Corvairs, and I can be an advocate for them, and be an advocate for people who are different. Like I planned. So it's really not changing what I want to do."

"It's not?" I thought it was changing a lot of very important things.

"No."

"You really want to live with Kenny?"

"Yes."

I eyed him. "You have thought about this, haven't you?"

He nodded.

"Why didn't you say anything to me?"

"Because I knew you wouldn't like it," he confessed. "And you don't like it. I can tell. You think I can't do it, or shouldn't do it."

He had read me perfectly.

"Lydia said I should tell you. She thinks it's a good plan."

I recalled again what Annie had told me so long ago. I would not change Benjy. He would change me.

I fished in my pocket, pulled out the keys to our Corvair, and placed them in his palm. "You'll need a car while you're living at Kenny's," I told him.

He eyed the keys, then me. "You won't have a Corvair, Dad," he said. "The Camry is not as good as the Corvair."

"I will have a Corvair. Because, if you do this, you have to promise me that I can have the first Corvair you restore. Is that a deal?"

He closed his fingers over the keys. "Deal," he agreed. "But you have to pay for it."

"I will pay for it," I assured him.

He beamed.

"You sold a lot of Corvairs today," I told him. "You're good at this."

He grinned brightly—brighter than he'd grinned in a long time.

I reached over and tousled his hair, and he didn't resist. "Do you remember when you opened the envelope from Wheeler?" I asked him. "Do you remember what you said?"

He nodded. Of course, he remembered.

But I still reminded him. "You said there was no place in this world for you. But you were wrong. There is a place. You're making it."

He nodded, then suddenly yanked me into a bear hug and squeezed, knocking half the wind out of me. I didn't care. Bless you, Lydia, for teaching him to hug.

The Corvair fired up on Benjy's first turn of the key. When we reached the cemetery gate, I thanked the manager for staying open. "Not a problem," he said. "I've been admiring your car. My grandparents had one. But haven't you heard? It's unsafe at any speed!" Then he winked.

Benjy understood the social cue. From deep in his gut, rolling up the back of his throat, then erupting out his wide open mouth, came a volcanic roar. "HA, HA, HA, HA!" he laughed, his body heaving. "HA, HA, HA, HA!" he rejoiced, proudly and defiantly different, rocking behind the wheel of his beloved Corvair.

ACKNOWLEDGMENTS

Many wonderful people urged me to write this book, and then supported me when I was on the verge of giving it up. I want to – and wish I could – thank each by name, but please accept my apologies in advance if lack of space, poor notes, or bad memory cause me to leave one of you out.

First, I thank Jonathan Rintels, Sr., my father, who first introduced me to Corvairs, and my son, Jonathan III, known to all as "J.B.," who first introduced me to Asperger's Syndrome. In truth, they both taught me so much more about life than they did about those two things, and they both continue to inspire me daily. And while the three generations of my family obviously informed this book, please understand that the Bennetts are a fictional family in a work of fiction, and the two families should not be confused.

Those who generously tutored me in all things Corvair include Scott Allison, Warren LeVeque, Michael LeVeque, Timothy Shortle, Wade Lanning, David Robertson, Allen Bristow, the other always supportive members of the Central Virginia Corvair Club, and the excellent *Communique* magazine of CORSA, the Corvair Society of America. Dollie Cole gave generously of her time to share stories about her late husband, Edward N. Cole, the "Father of the Corvair." George Bonfe, a wheelchair-bound Corvair owner and car restorer, kindly spent so much time with me, a total stranger; he deserves his own book.

On Asperger's, Patsy A. Dass, Ph.D., reviewed the manuscript and gave many excellent suggestions. The writings of John Elder Robison and Jonathan Mooney fascinated and inspired me. The dedicated faculty and staff at the Oakland School and at Monticello High School in Charlottesville, Virginia taught me so much as they successfully supported my son's education. The staff of the Virginia Youth Leadership Forum, a wonderful summer program in which special needs students are trained and motivated to become tomorrow's leaders, was amazing.

Michael Alan Eddy was the manuscript's first reader, and his uncharacteristically unrestrained enthusiasm sustained me through months of rewrites. Stefan Bechtel, Melinda Metz, J. B. Rintels, David Rintels, Vicki Riskin, Peter Loge, Charlie Clark, Scott Patton, Kate Moore Patton, Lynne W. Levine, Robert Bianco, Judith Fox, Dr. Lillian Carson, Dean Johnson, and many others gave so much of their time to share useful insights as well as unwavering support when I really needed it.

David Wilk offered me wise counsel about the publishing business, patiently answering my endless questions, and then offered to publish my book – every writer should be so lucky. Gary Hamburgh took the gorgeous cover photo, enthusiastically granted me permission to use it, and then after reading the manuscript sent me a note I will forever treasure.

Saving the most important for last, I thank both my children, J.B. and Elizabeth. You two are the best, period, end of story, and make me feel so blessed. Every father should be so lucky.